YOUR TRAIN IS RUN

Contents

PREFACE

When I was in primary school, we used to get many topics for essay writing. My most favorite topic was 'My Train Journey'. In those days, I used to write all the good things about the train journey. Following is an imaginary excerpt from an essay on 'My Train Journey'.

"I love traveling by trains. Last year, I got a chance to travel to my aunt's place by train. We boarded the train at Samastipur railway station and we were going to Darbhanga. When the train arrived on the platform, I was amazed to see the giant sized steam engine. It was looking like a black beauty. Some staffs from my father's office had come to help us in boarding the train. They arranged our luggage in the compartment. I was lucky to get a window seat; after a small round of fight with my younger brother and sister. When the train started running on the track, I was able to see the engine from the window. The engine was looking magnificent when it was belching black smoke from its chimney. The whistle of the train seemed like music to my ears. The rattling sound of the wheels was similar to the sounds of percussion instruments which are played along with song and music. Once the train stopped at a small station then my father bought peanuts for all of us. We spread a towel on the seat to keep the peanuts on it. We loved having those peanuts. The chutney further enhanced the taste of peanuts. ...."

Once I grew to become an adult, my love affair with train journeys dwindled with my advancing age. It was a pure coincidence that I landed in a job of a sales representative. The nature of my job involved too much travelling; that too by trains. Thus, over a period of time I was exposed to too much of the train journey. After spending more than a decade in my job in the sales, I am no longer in a position to say that I love to travel by train. I no more enjoy traveling at all. I just feel sick at the sight of a train approaching a platform.

When I was a student, the population of India was 700 million. It has grown to more than a billion now; meaning more than 300 million people have been added in this country. This is the main reason of the growing crowd in the trains. For me, a train journey is more a pain than a pleasure which does not allow me to hum the hit song from a 1970s Hindi movie. The song goes like this, "Gari bulaa rahi hai, seeti bajaa rahi hai."

This novel is about numerous problems which one has to face while traveling by a train. Nevertheless, people endure all the hardships because trains are the only affordable means to undertake long distance journey through a vast country like India.

1

The Holi Vacations

It was a cold December morning of Delhi. The famous winter of Delhi was at its peak. Rahul had barely mustered up courage to come out of bed so that he could fetch the newspaper from balcony. There was a gloomy view from the balcony. Everything was looking different shades of dull gray with a light touch of turquoise blue. The lanes and buildings appeared like sepia tinted scenes from some black and white movie. The fog was so dense that he could not see the houses more than two blocks away from his balcony. The small park; in front of his house; was looking mysterious because most of the trees were half emerging from misty fog. The railing of the balcony was so cold that it hurt to touch. Dew drops were dripping from the railing of the balcony. A solitary pigeon was sitting on the railing. The pigeon had fluffed up its body to beat the cold. In spite of the freezing cold, some ladies could be seen walking on the street. They were the maidservants who were on their way to do their job of cleaning and washing in different households of the colony. Rahul quickly shut the door and went back to the cozy comforts of his bedroom to enjoy the morning tea along with the smell of the fresh newspaper.

From his balcony, he entered his drawing room. The drawing room was about 15 feet long and 12 feet wide. A sofa set; with thick fabric on top; was kept in the drawing room. The sofa cover was of dark blue color; contrasting well with light cream walls. A carpet of artificial fabric was adorning the floor of the drawing room. The floral pattern on the carpet was run of the mill; as can be seen on many carpets sold by vendors roaming through the streets of different cities. A plastic table was serving the purpose of the centre table in the drawing room. A bulky TV was kept atop a table in one corner of the drawing room. Because of the cathode ray tube, the TV was taking too much of space. The top of the TV was adorned with a flower vase which was full of artificial flowers. One of the walls was adorned with some illustrations and paintings which were made by the lady of the house when she was yet to get married. One of the paintings showed a village belle lying on lush green lawns; with her back towards the sky. She was in the midst of writing a letter on a lotus leaf. A kid of deer was prancing nearby. Anybody could easily guess that the painting depicted Shakuntala; the lead protagonist from the famous novel by Kalidasa. Another wall hanging was made in the style of fresco with the help of cotton. The famous Taj Mahal was depicted in that fresco. Such paintings and

9

illustrations are quite common in many households. You will find common designs in all such paintings and illustrations because all of them are made for the sole purpose of impressing the family of the prospective groom; during negotiations for arranged marriage.

The kitchen was almost in the drawing room; with a small door working as a partition in between. Kitchen was long but not so wide but the long platform in the kitchen compensated by providing adequate space for keeping various items. Wooden cupboards could also be seen on the walls of the kitchen. In most of the modern flats, a kitchen always opens in the drawing room. This helps the lady of the house to keep talking to a guest while preparing tea and snacks for the guest. If looked from another perspective, it can be quite inconvenient to allow some unwanted guest in the drawing room because of the possible encroachment into privacy of the lady of the house. Kitchen and drawing room were followed by a narrow corridor which led to two bedrooms of the house.

Rahul's bedroom was about 12 feet long and 10 feet wide; a big size considering normally smaller sized rooms in rented flats. Walls were painted in dull cream. Some decoration was made on the ceiling with Plaster of Paris.

The baroque floral motif on the ceiling told about the cheap taste of the landlord of the house. Cheap ultra-small chandeliers were precariously suspended below bulb holders. The chandeliers were covered with a thick layer of black soot. It showed the disinterest which the current occupants of the house had in such useless decorations. A bathroom was attached to the bedroom; providing the much needed privacy to the occupants of that bedroom. A huge watercolor landscape adorned the wall. It showed the famous scene of Sita crossing the Lakshman Rekha; from the Ramayana. This painting was gifted to Rahul from his friend who is a painter but is not as famous as the Hussain or the Raza. Rahul had taken all the pains to preserve that painting by proper framing with a glass top; as per the instructions of his painter friend. The double bed was of dark brown color and had a minimalistic design. It was made of plywood with some solid wood for proper support. The feet of the bed showed some semblance of artistry in the form of floral engravings. A CFL bulb was radiating diffused light in the room. The date of guarantee; marked with black ink; could be still seen on the ceramic base of the CFL. Such dates are usually written by retailers when they sell a CFL. When CFLs were introduced in the market they found few takers because of hefty price compared to the price of incandescent bulbs. Retailers found out an innovative way to boost the sales; by giving the guarantee of replacement if the CFL goes kaput within a year. There was a turquoise blue steel almirah in one corner of the room. It was fitted with a big mirror as well. It was fabricated by local manufacturer; which is the norm in most of the households because very few people can afford the branded ones. There was a small rack in another corner. It was made of very thin metallic tubes and appeared quite rickety. The rack was full of items; like shaving kit, toothbrushes, soaps, shampoo, combs, first-aid kit, a bag-full of medicines, ear-buds, cell phone chargers and some cosmetics. Considering the shoddy quality of the rack; it was amazing to see its capacity to take so much of load. A washing machine was neatly fitted in one corner of the room; in the gap between the wall and the bed. It was duly covered with an old bed-sheet to prevent the dust from spoiling it. Rahul's bed showed tell-tale signs of well-deserved sleep of two adults. The bed-sheet was disheveled and the duvet was eager to fall off the bed; with a part of it covering the lower half of Rahul's body.

Rahul was living with his wife; Ankita and son Aryan. Rahul was in his mid thirties but looked as if he was in his late twenties. It was mainly because of his unblemished skin. He attributed it to a disciplined lifestyle; in terms of eating and drinking habits and a regular regimen of jogging and light exercise. But the habit of jogging did not come naturally to him. About seven years back he went to a doctor because of some health related issue. After a thorough checkup and many diagnostic tests, the doctor said him to run for his life. After that warning call from the doctor, Rahul fell in line and began to follow a strict regimen.

If any of you is following a strict regimen of early morning jogging or walking, you may have observed that majority of the morning walkers are above forty. Majority of people start taking jogging as a serious business only when a doctor tells them, "Bhaag Milkha Bhaag (Run for your life Milkha)."

His head was still covered with decent amount of hair; although baldness ran in his family. His face was adorned with small eyes, small but pointed nose and full lips. His wife sometimes felt envious of his luscious lips. His clean-shaven look was accentuated by early morning stubble. His wife; Ankita was about five years younger to him. Compared to somewhat square and muscular frame of Rahul, she was rather thin in appearance. Many people gawked at her lean and thin frame even after a decade of her marriage. Many people still confuse her to be a college student. She does not need to take much effort in maintaining a decent figure rather she attributed it to her genes. Her mother, maternal aunt, father, uncles and brothers; everyone is naturally lean and thin and no one ever needed to worry about accumulating fat on the body. Thus, Ankita too looks much younger than her real age. Her round face is adorned with big eyes and heavy eyelashes, small nose and ultrathin lips. Her eyelashes make everyone envious whenever she goes to a beauty parlor. Her fair skin proved to be asset while her parents were trying to find a suitable match for her. It is another matter that the inhabitants of the subcontinent are seldom fair. Most of them are different shades of brown; right from dark brown to light brown. People whose skin resembles that of the color of a wheat grain are usually termed as fair-skinned people in our country. Aryan is 8 years old but his growth is very good. He looks much taller than boys of his age. Many friends and relatives always comment that he looks like a photocopy of Rahul; in terms of stocky frame but his nose and eyes resemble her mother's. His cherubic face is quite normal for a child of his age but he has oodles of love handles. This can be attributed to the fact that most of the urban couples now-a-days have either one or two children. Parents focus all their attention, energy and resources to the ultra-small brood of their children. This has translated in better nutrition for middle class children; which is manifested in good growth in children who were born in post-liberalization India. The situation was different during 1970s and 1980s. Most of the families had at least four children, while some daredevils even maintained families of six to seven children. Homemakers of the 21st century India would fail to understand the finance management practices of big families of the seventies or eighties.

Rahul had just begun to glance through the headlines. Ankita was sitting beside him; browsing through the colorful supplement of the newspaper. Both of them were enjoying the morning tea. Aryan also joined them. He came with his notebook and said, "Papa, do you know that I have won the first prize in an essay competition in my class?"

Rahul said with some enthusiasm, "Hmm! That is great. Well done. What was the topic of the essay?"

Aryan proudly said, "We had to write an essay on 'My Train Journey'. See the certificate and medal which I got as a winner."

Ankita hugged her son and Rahul gave a peck on his forehead. Ankita said, "Wow, this shows that he is really my son."

Rahul said, "When he does some nasty things then he becomes my son. But the moment he excels in some competition he becomes your son. You are really clever."

Rahul then said to Aryan, "That's great my son. Can we have a look at what you wrote in the essay?"

Aryan opened his notebook and showed the page on which the essay was written. The excerpt of the essay is as follows:

"I love traveling by trains. My teacher says that trains connect the people of India. This essay is about my train journey from Delhi to Shimla. I went on that journey with my classmates and class-teacher. We took this journey at the beginning of summer vacations. My father dropped me to school at five in the morning and then all the students of my class took a bus to reach Delhi station. We boarded the Delhi Kalka Shatabdi Express. Our journey started at 7:45 AM. Shatabdi express is a beautiful train. All the coaches have air-conditioned chair cars. The train was neat and clean. Seats were very large and comfortable. The moment our train left Delhi all of us were served breakfast in the train by the train staffs. We were served butter toast, omlette and Swiss rolls. We were also served tea and coffee. They also gave mineral water to each passenger. All the passengers were given newspaper as well. The train was running very fast. All of us were thrilled at seeing the speed of the train. The train took just four hours to cover a distance of about 300 km to reach Kalka. After getting down at Kalka, we boarded a toy train to Shimla. The toy train had small coaches. We enjoyed sitting in that train. The speed of the toy train was much less than the speed of Shatabdi Express. We could see beautiful hills and mountains all around. We also saw lush green forests along the hills. The weather was comfortable even during the month of June. Our class-teacher bought packets of chips and cakes for all of us. We played the game of Antakshari while on our way to Shimla. The beautiful toy train, matched with the beautiful hills of the area. ...."

When Rahul finished reading that essay, Ankita said to Rahul, "You know what? This essay has kindled a desire in me. I want to celebrate this year's Holi at my parents' place."

Rahul was still looking at the newspaper but said, "But what is wrong in celebrating Holi with me? We also celebrate Holi in a decent way here at Delhi."

Ankita said, "Did I tell you that I would be going alone? I will go along with you and Aryan. All of us should go together. That would be nice because we shall be visiting my parents' place after so many years."

Rahul said, "But you know that I hate traveling. Why are you forcing me to take such a long journey?"

Ankita said, "Yeah, I know that you hate traveling. But I enjoy traveling and so does Aryan. You are no more living a bachelor's life. You are a married person with a family. You need to take interest in our interests."

Rahul said, "But Holi is in March and this is still December. What is the need for making advance plan? We will give a well deserved thought to this issue at an appropriate time."

Aryan also joined their conversation, "I know you. You always try to confuse us by your glib talks. I also want to go to the grandpa's village. I simply love to play there."

Ankita said, "He is right. He gets plenty of space to play in the village. This is not possible in this cramped space of our two BHK (Bedroom Hall Kitchen) flat. I cannot allow him to play on the street because that is not safe. So many teenagers keep racing on their bikes. Do you know Chiku; the son of our neighbor Sharmaji? Last week, he was hit by a bike and got badly injured."

Rahul said, "Yeah, you are right. Even the nearby park is not safe; with so many drug addicts hanging around."

While they were discussing about their plan for the Holi vacations, Rahul's mobile phone started playing some catchy number from Bollywood. It was a call from his in-laws. His father-in-law was on the line.

Rahul picked up the phone and said, "Pranam! Papa, how are you?"

His father-in-law said, "I am fine. I have called you to invite you for the festival of Holi. Why don't you spend this year's Holi with us? Many years have passed when you last came to our village. Many people are eagerly waiting to meet you. I have not seen Aryan since a long time. He must have grown very big by now. "

Rahul said, "Err! But I will be too busy during February and March. I have to discuss appraisal with my colleagues."

Rahul's father-in-law said, "I am not going to hear any excuse. You have to come for Holi at any cost."

Rahul has had enough pressure from all sides and had no other way than to give his assent. He said, "Ok, we will be coming for the festival of Holi."

After their telephonic conversation was over, Rahul said to Ankita, "You should be happy now. I can smell some deeper conspiracy hatched by you and your father."

Ankita flashed a wide smile. Her crooked canine teeth further enhanced her beauty. She said, "What is wrong in conspiring against my husband when the purpose is to visit my parents."

Aryan was just jumping with joy, "In Delhi, I don't get to play Holi with children of my age. In front of all the grown up people, I have to behave like a nice boy. At the village, I really enjoy playing Holi; with so many children of my age for company."

Rahul said, "But be careful. Last time, you slipped while trying to climb a guava tree. Children of your age are not fit enough for such adventures. When I was of your age, I used to climb a guava tree like an ace professional. "

Rahul further said, "Do you know Ankita? Soon after getting down from the bus, I used to run towards the big orchard surrounding our huge house. I, my brother and my sisters; all of us just raced to come first at climbing the guava tree. I still get the fond memories of sweet and juicy guavas in my mouth."

Ankita said, "But today's children are not so lucky. They have so much pressure for study that they seldom get time to enjoy those luxuries which we enjoyed as children. I loved playing in the river for hours. No modern water park can give the joy which a pond or a river in a village could."

Aryan said, "But I love running through the green farms whenever I get a chance to go to the village. I hope to learn how to climb a guava tree during this trip. Children of our age enjoy playing games on computer and smartphones. You won't understand; as you are still stuck in simple games; like Pokemon."

Aryan further said, "I have seen your river in the village. It is so filthy that I won't dare to even dip my feet in it. Water parks are more hygienic. You also get nice swimming costumes to wear. They also sell burgers and pizza at the water parks. Can you get those things near your river?"

Ankita tried to bring back Rahul on the main topic, "It appears that you will be wasting your time in silly talks. Why don't you try to book a ticket for our journey?"

Rahul said, "Relax, it is still the month of December. Holi is probably on the sixth of March. You know that there is a two-month window for booking advance ticket. So, we cannot book a ticket before the first week of January."

Ankita said, "You can at least check the position of waiting list in some trains. That would give us a fair idea of the possible rush."

Rahul said, "Should we take a direct train to Darbhanga or should we go via Patna?"

Ankita replied, "A direct train would be better. Traveling from Patna to Darbhanga is not easy; especially during festival rush. It is tough to get a seat in overcrowded buses. I have heard that the Patna Bus Stand has been shifted and is now quite far from the railway station. The private taxis just resort to extortion to cash on the festival rush."

Rahul got up from the bed and rushed to the bathroom. Meanwhile, he told Aryan, "Aryan, can you switch the computer on."

After coming back from the bathroom, Rahul sat near his desktop. He opened the railways' website to check the status. He said, "It is showing the status till last week of February. The waiting list for sleeper class is running into 300 plus to 400 plus. Even in AC classes, the situation is not good. I don't know how some people manage to take leave so much in advance."

After checking the status for train tickets, Rahul got ready for his office. He was wearing a dark trouser and a shirt with white and light blue stripes. He put on the black shoes which were gleaming because of a fresh coat of polish. He also put on a dark blue blazer with red tie to complement the look. The brass buttons on his blazer were sparkling with light.

Looking at his dress, Ankita said, "You will always remain somewhat orthodox when dressing for your office. This plain red tie has gone out of fashion. You should try the latest design of ties."

Rahul said, "Come on, I am just going to my office and not to a cocktail party. I know how to dress for the occasion."

When Rahul sat on the sofa for breakfast, he found a sumptuous fare in front of him. The plastic table served as the dining table as well as the centre table as per the need. The aloo-paratha (bread stuffed with mashed potato) had ghee dripping from all over. The vegetable curry was extra spicy with tender pieces of cauliflower and potato. The omlette was full of finely chopped spring onions which emanated a heady aroma. Ankita also served kheer for desert. Rahul just gorged on the breakfast. He said, "I will get you a monthly season ticket from Delhi to Darbhagna if you promise to make such tasty breakfast every day."

Ankita did not say anything but just smiled. When Rahul was leaving for office, he said to Aryan, "Enjoy your winter vacation. You can tell the whole world that you are going to meet your Nana and Nani during Holi."

2

Bujhaavan And His Friends

Bujhaavan Manjhi is home after a hard day at work. He is a daily wage earner whose work depends on the opportunity he gets. The past season had been good for him because he could get to work on a construction site. He has saved enough money that he can afford to go to his village in Bihar to celebrate Holi with his family.

Bujhavan Manjhi lives in the south western part of Delhi. He is living in a rented accommodation where he shares a room with three other guys. His room is ten feet wide and twelve feet long; which is a luxury given the prevalence of much smaller rooms in the slum where he lives. The slum has one hundred such rooms. The rooms are arranged in rows of ten each. Each room has a door and a small window. The roof is made up of corrugated asbestos sheets which make it for tortuous living during the peak summer. Most of the inhabitants in this slum are migrant laborers from Bihar and UP. While some of them live alone, many others live with their families. There are two toilets to serve the need of about five hundred people. But people prefer to live in this slum because many other slums in the locality do not provide toilet facilities. There are two taps from the Delhi Jal Board to fulfill the need of water for the slum-dwellers. Most of the people in this slum get up early in the morning to beat the heavy rush at the toilets and at the water taps.

While cooking dinner, Bujhaavan said to his room-mates, "Hey, what have you planned for Holi?"

One of his roommates; Jitan; belongs to the same village. He said, "I would love to go to the village. But I don't want to go alone."

Bujhaavan asked, "You are a grown up man. Why are you afraid of going alone?"

Jitan said, "Going alone involves lot of problems. You always run the risk of being duped by the ticket checkers, railway police, coolies and touts during the journey. There is an additional risk of getting robbed by petty criminals who often pose as fellow passengers."

Bujhavan said, "I have already planned for celebrating Holi at the village. We can go together."

His other roommates; Ramchander and Narayan; said in a chorus, "That sounds good. We would also like to go with you. After all, our village is your neighboring village and a neighbor should always help his neighbor."

Once they were through with the cooking, Jitan took out stainless steel plates for everyone. The pressure cooker and the wok served as platter. They used the ladles as serving spoons to take out rice and vegetable curry. Bujhaavan was the first to be served for being the eldest of the lot. He is in his late thirties. Jitan is five years younger to him. Ramchander and Narayan were in their early twenties. Bujhaavan is of short height; just a little taller than five feet. He is dark skinned. His face is somewhat round with sunken eyes, small but thick nose and even thicker lips. His hairs are straight but disheveled because of lack of hair care. He also sports a thick moustache; like the movie stars of the south Indian cinema. Jitan, Ramchander and Narayan are almost of the same height as Bujhaavan; and all of them are dark skinned. Jitan's face is somewhat similar to that of Bujhaavan but the upper incisors are always flashing out of his mouth. Narayan and Ramchander are lanky fellows with sunken cheeks and prominent cheekbones. Their noses are small and wide but their lips are full. All of them have the same surname, i.e. Manjhi. They belong to the lowest of the lower castes; called Musahar. The Musahars come under the Scheduled Castes and are mainly found in Bihar.

27

They are not associated with any particular job related to their caste; unlike some other lower castes. Because of abject poverty; many people from this caste are often forced to eat rats. Rat is known as musaa in many dialects of Bihar and hence the name Musahar is supposed to have evolved from this fact.

Narayan and Ramchander were playing the role of the younger brothers while the food was being served. All of them have been living in Delhi since last five years and are living like a closely knit family; sharing their sorrows and happiness.

Many examples of such ghettos can be found in most of the big cities. Laborers often prefer to live in such ghettos because of perceived guarantee of living in a cocoon made of similar people; in terms of socio-economic background, caste and place of origin. This trend is not limited to poor people only. This can be seen in case of students; who come from different states to prepare for various competitive examinations. This trend is also evident among middle class people who migrate to big cities in search of better prospects. While the laborers may get the benefit of some degree of social security while living in ghettos, students often suffer because of it. A student; living in a ghetto; may not get the much desired opportunity to interact with a diverse set of people and may end up being a loser in the sweepstakes.

While taking a morsel, Narayan asked, "Bhaiya Bujhaavan, I did not understand it. Holi is in March and it is still December. Then why are we discussing about the Holi vacations? Isn't it too early?"

Bujhavan answered the way any wise man would, "This is the right time to plan for Holi. Do you know that you can book your train tickets two months in advance? If we want to start on the first of March then we need to book a ticket on the first of January. Otherwise it will be too late. All tickets get booked within a few minutes of opening of the bookings. During Holi and Chhath, everybody appears to be headed towards Bihar."

Jitan came with his opinions, "Do you remember the scene when we were going to our village for the Chhath about two years back. We faced too many problems."

Narayan said, "Yes, we did not have reserved tickets. We had to travel in the general compartment. It was difficult to even enter the compartment. We paid hundred rupees per person and only then the coolie allotted us the seats. I had to control my bladder throughout the journey."

Ramchander said, "The coach was packed with people. It was impossible to move even an inch from our seat. I almost peed in my pants but was able to jump out of the coach just in time when the train had stopped at a small station."

After finishing their dinner, they were busy in arranging their beds. There were four folding cots in the room. Cots were made of iron frames and thick ribbons of plastic. All the cots were arranged in a row to make a huge bed. The winter season made it feasible for them to share a huge bed. There was a single bulb in the room which was switched off by Narayan. The light from the streetlight was coming inside the room and it was way too much for their comfort. Jitan covered the window with a towel to minimize the glare from the streetlight. After that they could get a diffused light which was serving the purpose of a night lamp.

While they were lying in the comfortable warmth of the quilt, Bujhaavan said to Ramchander, "Have you seen the shop of the local travel agent? He books railway tickets. Your first task for tomorrow is to talk to him about the tickets. Try to drive hard bargain from him. He is an expert at extortion."

Next day, Bujhaavan went for work at around eight in the morning. Jitan and Narayan went to the nearby crossroads which is popularly known as the 'Labor Chowk'. Many laborers throng this place early in the morning in the hope of finding some work. They are always willing to do any task to earn a day's wages. They consider it as a boon when someone agrees to pay the minimum wages as specified by the government. But most of the time, they have to settle for lesser amount. People come there looking for laborers for different kinds of task. It can be as simple task as cleaning the overhead water tank, clearing the weeds from the garden, cleaning the rooftop, etc. Sometimes, someone may also get to work for repairing a leaking roof, or fixing the plaster of the walls or cleaning the windows in high-rise apartments.

There was a huge crowd of laborers at the Labor Chowk. Most of the laborers were sitting on their haunches, while some others were either standing still or taking a leisurely stroll. All of them were on the sides of the road; trying to avoid getting hit by speeding cars and bikes. The moment some car stopped, it ended up being surrounded by many hopeful laborers. The scene at the 'Labor Chowk' was reminiscent of the early days of the Industrial Revolution. In England and America, people used to converge near the port in the hope of getting a work for the day. According to the books on business management, things changed after Henry Ford introduced his theories on operations management. But India is a unique country where you can get to view different stages of development; right from primitive to the modern; in every aspect of life. On the one hand, you get to see prospective employees searching for jobs on various job portals and on the other, you get to see people thronging a crossroads in hope of finding a day's work. Most of the laborers are still the generalists rather than being specialists in a particular task. As there is no guarantee of finding a work of choice, so the laborers find no incentive in becoming specialist at any particular task. When finding a job is still an issue; there is no point of thinking about various issues of social security and safety at the workplace. Situation is no different even for majority of people who go on to take some technical degree. We can easily see many engineers landing the job of sales representative.

Ramchander went to the travel agent's shop at about ten. The travel agent's shop is in a small market complex on the main road. This market complex has twenty shops. The shops are made in two rows; with some space in between for parking of two-wheelers. The travel agent's shop is a ten feet long and eight feet wide room. A small table; made of wooden board is at the centre. A high-back swiveling chair with faux-leather cover adorns the space behind the table. Some plastic chairs are kept near the entrance for customers. A small idol of Lakshmi Ganesh could be seen on a niche on the wall behind the high-back chair. A zero watt bulb was radiating red light above the idols. Fresh flowers in front of the idol showed that the travel agent had finished his routine of worshipping the goddess of wealth. The travel agent is about twenty five years old. He is tall and well built. His bulging biceps show that he is a regular visitor to the neighborhood gym. His Mohawk haircut is in tune with the latest trend. He is wearing a skin-tight low-cut jeans and a body hugging T-shirt. A thick necklace of gold is clinging around his neck. When Ramchander said to him about his travel plan, the travel agent said in typical Haryanvi accent, "Hmm! A train ticket to Bihar and that too during Holi. That is difficult but I can manage it. From your dress it appears that you may not be in a position to pay the excess money required for getting a confirmed ticket. Why don't you go by the general class?"

Ramchander tried to sound confident and said, "No! No! It is not like that. We also know the situation. We have planned for some extra money in our travel budget. Don't worry about that."

The travel agent smelt some blood and said, "At present the rate for a confirmed ticket is Rs. 1000 extra apart from charges for the ticket."

Ramchander's confident stance gave way to somewhat flexible look. He said, "What are you talking? You will get many rich customers from whom you can make money. Have some pity on us. We are poor laborers. We cannot afford to pay so much of extra money. Cannot you adjust a little bit?"

The travel agent said, "I told you earlier. Why don't you try to go to your village during off season? In that case, I charge only a hundred rupees for my services."

Ramchander said, "Sir, how will you feel when you will have to spend an important festival without your family? Just think about our children. Just think about the happiness which you can bring for our family. Don't be so heartless and have some pity for poor people."

The travel agent then said, "Ok! This is my final offer. I will take five hundred rupees for each confirmed ticket. Don't try to argue with me after this. This is my last offer."

Ramchander said, "But Sir................."

The travel agent interrupted, "Don't waste my time. I have to attend to other customers as well."

Suddenly, the mobile phone of the travel agent started ringing and he became busy in answering that call. Sensing his mood, Ramchander said, "Ok, go ahead and book our tickets."

After that, the travel agent noted down the names and other details of the wannabe passengers. Then the travel agent told to Ramchander, "It is 25th December today. I will be booking your tickets on the 1st of January. Don't forget to pay at least a thousand rupees as advance before first January. Give me a reminder on the 31st. You can collect your ticket any time on first January after paying the rest of the money."

Ramchander was feeling happy at getting a good deal from the travel agent. When he shared the news with others in the evening, Bujhaavan was not happy. Bujhaavan said, "You will never learn the ways of this world. Had I been in your place, I would not have settled for a single penny more than rupees three hundred. Nevertheless, since you have finalized the deal you can go ahead. Pay some advance to that travel agent."

Jitan asked from Bujhavan, "But you have not told about the train which we shall be taking for our journey."

Narayan said, "I think Freedom Fighter would be better. It leaves Delhi at about eight in the evening. It will allow us to utilize a full day to earn some money. Traveling by any other train entails taking a day off because other trains depart during the day."

Bujhaavan said, "He is right. Moreover, Freedom Fighter reaches Darbhanga in the afternoon which will allow us to get a bus to our village."

On the first of January; all of them reached the travel agent's shop early. It was seven in the morning. The travel agent was about to open his shop. Looking at them he said, "Hey! You guys seem to be in a hurry. Once you have paid advance to me there is no need to come. You are not going to board your train from my shop."

Narayan said, "Actually we were worried about the tickets. We thought that seeing our face would work as good reminder for you. We were afraid that you may forget our case if you get a fat cat for air-conditioned classes."

The travel agent said, "Hey buddy, every customer is equal for me. I don't discriminate on the basis of sleeper or air-conditioned classes. Once I promise a customer I take all the efforts to ensure a ticket. I have connections at the top level in the rail ministry. Don't worry once you have reached my shop."

The online booking opens at eight in the morning. The travel agent was sitting in front of his computer. Bujhaavan, Jitan, Ramchander and Narayan were sitting in front of him; craning their necks to see the changing colors of the computer screen. He quickly called a nearby tea-seller and asked him to serve tea to the new customers. The tea-seller came with a kettle and a bunch of disposable glasses. After putting four disposable glasses on the table, he poured the steaming hot brew in those glasses. While the travel agent was furiously typing on the keyboard and clicking the mouse button, all four were looking at his face with a heavy sense of anticipation. A few moments later, the travel agent announced, "Congratulations! You have got confirmed tickets."

All the four guys jumped in excitement, "Hurray! We got a ticket for Holi. It sounds great."

The travel agent said, "Your train is Freedom Fighter. You have got birth numbers 7,8, 15 and 16 in the coach S7. All your births are side births. Here are printouts for your ticket. I am giving four printouts as bonus. Happy?"

Bujhaavan became somewhat emotional, "Thank you Sahib. Two years have passed when I last met my wife and children. It is only because of you that I will be going to my village this Holi. I know how difficult it can be to get a confirmed ticket during the festival of Holi."

After that, Bujhaavan held the travel agent's hands and kissed them with a deep sense of gratitude. Jitan, Ramchander and Narayan followed the suit. Within a flash, Narayan ran a short sprint to the sweetmeat shop and came with a small packet of laddoos. He stuffed the first laddoo in the travel agent's mouth and shared the remaining laddoos with his room-mates. For most of the people, going to their hometown can be a matter of celebration; especially when the purpose of the visit is some festival or some family function.

As it was the New Year Day so all of them had taken a day off from their work. They are among some of the lucky guys who don't need to submit a leave application for availing a leave. This is one of the very few luxuries which a daily wage earner can afford to enjoy. The confirmed tickets in their hands further emboldened their plans to enjoy the New Year Day with full vigor. They went back to their rooms as it was too early for the shops to open. They washed their clothes, cleaned their room and took bath. Narayan was humming a song while he was taking bath. One of his neighbors asked, "Hey Narayan, you appear to be in a jovial mood. What's up?"

Narayan replied, "Yeah! We are going to our village during Holi. Today, we got success in getting confirmed tickets for our journey."

The neighbor said, "Then there must be a party tonight in your room. Can we get an invitation?"

Narayan said, "Yes, but the invitation is only for those who can come with a confirmed ticket to show as a proof of journey. The quartet of my room is enough for a grand party."

During afternoon, they went to the bazaar to make arrangements for their party. Their first stop was the mutton shop. Narayan asked, "Bujhaavan Bhaiya, how much mutton should we buy?"

Bujhaavan said, "Not less than two kilos."

Ramchander said, "That would be too much for us."

Jitan said, "This is a New Year party and we can easily finish everything. You are not aware of the appetite Bujhaavan and Narayan."

After buying mutton, they moved on to a shop which sells country liquor. While they were buying a bottle for each, Narayan said, "Sometimes I get a dream of sipping the foreign liquor in a beautiful glass tumbler."

Hearing that, Bujhaavan said, "Within six months' time I will be promoted to the rank of supervisor at the construction site. I will serve foreign liquor when I will throw a party on my promotion. All your dreams shall be fulfilled on that day. Till then, let us manage with this country liquor."

Once they had purchased the liquor, Narayan asked, "We also need to buy some rice, cooking oil and spices. Where should we go for this?"

Bujhaavan said, "We can only go to Shankar General Stores. Do we have a choice on this matter?"

Ramchander said, "That shop is owned by the son of our landlord. We have to follow his dictum because we are not allowed to buy anything from any other shop."

Narayan said, "Yeah, last week he caught me while I was buying a packet of biscuits from another shop. He did not think twice before slapping me really hard."

Bujhaavan said, "We should be happy that he is only forcing us to buy from his shop. He is at least not charging extra price for anything. One of my friends lives in another nearby slum. His landlord charges extra price for everything."

Once they were back from shopping, everybody was busy doing preparations for the dinner. Narayan took out stainless steel glasses and made drinks for the quartet. Ramchander borrowed a small speaker from one of his neighbors. He connected the speaker to his mobile phone. The speaker was now playing hit numbers from Hindi movies. Narayan was chopping the onions, Ramchander was grinding the spices and Jitan was kneading the dough. All this while, Bujhaavan was washing the mutton and utensils. The cots were folded to make enough room for a grand party. A carpet was neatly laid on one side of the room and all of them were sitting on the carpet. The rickety gas stove was composed of a small red cylinder with a burner at the top. It was proving somewhat difficult to balance the heavy wok atop the burner-cylinder combination. Within no time the room was filled with stench of alcohol, smoke of cigarettes and heady aroma of spices being sautéed. The tiny speaker was trying its best to produce optimum decibel to be in tune with the mood of the party. By the time they finished their first pegs, the day gave way to the night. It was dark outside and gates of most of the rooms were shut because of the cold weather. A few kids of the slum, however, were showing the audaciousness to peek inside Bujhaavan's room to kill their curiosity. But those kids were promptly shooed off by the vigilant eyes of the quartet. Bujhaavan took out some pieces of mutton fry and put them in front of his roommates.

Taking a bite from the piping hot piece of mutton, Jitan said, "Great taste. After my wife, if I love someone's culinary skills then it is you. Had it been a female instead of you then I would have kissed her hands."

Ramchander said, "Bujhaavan Bhaiya, be careful of his advances. He can be a dangerous person."

Bujhaavan smiled and said, "I know him since my childhood. I have full faith on him. I know that he is a straight guy and doesn't pursue the favorite hobby of nawabs."

Once Bujhaavan was through with cooking the mutton, it was time for Jitan to cook parathas. He was an expert with the rolling board and pin. While he was rolling paper thin layers for the parathas, Ramchander was helping with cooking those parathas.

Once the food was cooked, it was quickly served on the carpet. The wok was again serving as platter, while newspaper sheets were working as makeshift dinner plates. All of them just attacked on the finger licking stuff. Within no time, they easily gobbled the huge quantity of two kilos of mutton. They must have eaten at least forty parathas along with that.

After finishing the dinner, everyone was lying on the cot and generating different sounds of burps. Some of them were also using toothpicks to take out mutton fibres from their teeth. While they were making expert comments on the quality and taste of the food, Bujhaavan came with a new demand. He said, "I have heard that Narayan is a good dancer. Can he present a dance for all of us?"

Everybody clapped in support and cheered for Narayan. Narayan promptly jumped on the dance floor, i.e. on the carpet and began making dance moves. He was real expert in aping the dance moves of many hit numbers. Everybody else was clapping, whistling and giving catcalls on the live performance. The dance show must have continued for about ten minutes when someone knocked at the door.

The dance came to an abrupt halt. They hurriedly hid their glasses and bottles behind a huge carton. After that, Bujhaavan opened the door to find that it was the son of the landlord. He was leaning against the bonnet of his huge SUV. The fancy fog-lights atop the SUV were flashing blinding light. The silhouette of the huge SUV and the burly guy was looking too imposing against the glare. He appeared to be angry and said, "Have you lost all your senses. You should know that you are living among gentlemen of the society. Why are you creating so much of ruckus?"

Bujhaavan tried to smile as wide as he could and presented all his dentures at the service of the landlord's son. He barely managed to speak, "Err, actually, Umm! We were just enjoying the New Year Party. You know this Narayan. He is still immature. I know he crossed the limits tonight. Don't worry, I will talk to him. I can assure you that it is not going to happen in future."

Narayan interrupted in between and said, "What is wrong in enjoying the New Year Day? Even you guys hire DJs to enjoy your party."

The landlord's son grabbed Narayan's collar and gave him a tight slap. Narayan was almost shaking because of the shock treatment. The landlord's son said, "How dare you try to comment on my lifestyle. Don't forget that I am the landlord and you are the tenant. Nobody in this slum dares to look directly into my eyes. If you want to prolong your stay in this slum then behave the way I want you to behave."

Bujhaavan immediately fell on the feet of landlord's son and tried to pacify the matter, "Sir, he is an immature guy. He has yet to learn the ways of this world. I have been living under your protection since so many years. Nobody dares to mess with me because of the fact that I am your tenant. Please forgive him for his blunder."

With adequate amount of pressure released from his safety valves; the landlord's son calmed down a little and said, "Ok, take care that it does not happen in future. You know my record. I don't take time in throwing bad tenants from my house."

Once the landlord's son was gone, they bolted the door from inside. Looking at his face, Ramchander said, "I cannot see a mark of the slap on your face. He was mild while venting his frustration. Don't worry. Your face appears to be in perfect shape."

After that they enjoyed a hearty laugh. They said in unison, "When these rich guys keep on making noise with DJs throughout the night they never think about our comfort. We know that a poor person does not even have the right to enjoy a New Year Party."

Next morning, Narayan said, "How are we going to inform our family about our travel plan?"

Bujhaavan said, "Some rich people in my village have mobile phones even for the ladies in their house. I have the number of the wife of our Yadav neighbor. I will call on her number and will request her to call my wife. Once I will convey this to my wife, she will go to your village to tell your wife."

Narayan said with some tone of excitement, "That sounds good. Please call her now."

Bujhaavan called on the number of that lady and said, "Hello! It is me; Bujhaavan Manjhi. Yes! Yes! Bujhaavan from Delhi."

Covering the mobile phone with his hand, he whispered to his friends, "It appears that she has recognized me."

Then Bujhaavan continued on the phone, "Can you do me a favor? Can you call my wife? I need to talk to her. It is urgent."

The lady asked him to call after five minutes and disconnected the phone. Bujhaavan called again on that number after about five minutes. Now, he was talking to his wife, "Hello! Chhamiya. This is me; the father of your children."

Chhamiya was too shy to talk to her husband in front of other people. She could barely speak and said, "Hmm! Yes,

Yes. How are you? I was waiting for a call from you; the father of my Lattu."

Bujhaavan said, "There is good news. I am coming to celebrate the festival of Holi with you and our children. Jitan, Ramchander and Narayan are also coming. Please go to their houses and convey this news to them also. Take care, bye."

Chhamiya said, "Ok, I will tell them. Bye."

3

Aryan's Chacha (Uncle)

Rahul's brother lives in the same colony. His name is Rakesh and he lives just two blocks after Rahul's house. Rakesh's family includes his wife Poonam, a sixteen year old daughter Antara and an eight year old son Samaksh. Rahul's mother lives with Rakesh. Rahul's mother stays for a few days at Rahul's house from time to time. But she prefers to live with Rakesh because she has been living with him for a pretty long time. She probably feels more comfortable in the company of Rakesh and his family. She enjoys endless quarrels with Rakesh's children over the ownership of remote control. While Samaksh always wants to watch cartoons, his Dadi wants to watch soap operas. When she comes to stay with Rahul then Aryan tries to be formal with her because he has never lived with her. He always gives remote control to his Dadi. But the Dadi does not get the kick because she does not get a chance to fight with him the way she fights with Rakesh's children.

When Rahul came back from the office in the evening, they went to meet Rakesh and his family. The lane in which Rahul lives, has seen many recent developments; in the form of new shops coming up on the ground floor of almost every house. There are three shops; in a row; in front of his house. The shop at the left sells stationery items, the one at the middle sells and services air-conditioners and the shop on the right sells items of daily needs. A couple of eateries have also mushroomed in this lane. So, the residential area is gradually turning into a bazaar; resulting in more chaos which may not be good for a residential area. Opening of shops has provided some sort of convenience because you can get an item by literally dropping a shopping bag from your balcony. But you have to pay the price in the form of congestion, chaos and filth all around.

This is a big problem in almost every city of India. Most of the development is unplanned. People just open shops in each and every lane and along each and every road. We have read in our history books about the river valley civilizations. Now-a-days, it appears to be the era of 'Road-Side Civilization'. Once congestion in a city becomes unbearable, the authorities create a bypass road so that heavy vehicles can bypass the congested roads of the city. But within five or ten years, new houses and buildings come up along the bypass road. Gradually, shops and other business establishments also come up; creating further congestion; necessitating the construction of another bypass road. This is happening even in Delhi because most of the colonies are unauthorized developments.

After walking for about a couple of minutes, they reached Rakesh's house. Rakesh lives in a flat on the second floor. The entrance to his house is through a narrow lane. A heavy gate of iron guards the way to the staircase. The gate can be easily opened even from the outside. After climbing many steps, they were in front of the door to Rakesh's flat. Aryan pressed the call bell button which was near the top right corner of the door. Hearing the call-bell, Poonam opened the door. Poonam exchanged smiles with Rahul, Ankita and Aryan and let them in.

Once he entered his Chacha's house, Aryan started playing with Samaksh. Antara got an instruction to keep an eye on both the boys to prevent them from getting out of control. All the adults took their seats on the sofa set. The sofa set had maroon cover of a thick fabric. The heavy sofa set was occupying almost the whole space in the drawing room; with a small space in the middle for a carpet. The kitchen was on the right side, near the entrance to the house. The kitchen appeared like a narrow alley with a very long platform for keeping the gas stove and utensils. A maroon-colored refrigerator was kept opposite to the slab; leaving a narrow walkway which was barely enough for one person's comfort. A 60 inch LED TV was fixed on the wall opposite the entrance door of the drawing room. A huge wall clock was giving company to the television. There were two doors on the far end of the drawing room; each door leading to separate bedrooms. The door to the common bathroom was on the wall which ran along the kitchen. The opposite door in the drawing room opened to a large balcony. Thick curtains were covering almost all the doors and windows in the balcony. In spite of that, there was plenty of natural light in the room.

Rakesh is five years older than Rahul but looks much older because of a bald pate. He has thoroughly inherited the gene of baldness from his forefathers. Rahul's mother is in her seventies but is a sprightly old lady. She was showing all the energy while serving water to Rahul and his wife. Poonam switched the gas burner on to prepare tea for all of them. She asked Rahul, "By the way, what should I make for dinner?"

Rahul said, "No need to take too much pain for dinner. But it would be nice if you can make chicken biryani for us. It has been a long time when I last enjoyed the chicken biryani made by you. You possess some magic in your hands which shows in the food you make."

Rakesh called the chicken seller on his mobile phone and ordered a whole chicken. Hearing that, Rahul said, "Why are you ordering a whole chicken? Tell him to send only leg pieces instead."

Aryan also shouted, "Yes, I only love leg pieces. Other pieces from a chicken are not good."

Rakesh then told the chicken seller to supply only leg pieces.

After that, he asked Ankita, "All of you appear to be very happy today. There must be some good news."

Ankita said; while arranging biscuits and snacks on the table, "In fact, my father called early in the morning. He wants us to celebrate Holi at my village. We are planning to go to Simri for Holi vacations."

Poonam; who was standing with a tray in her hand; said, "It sounds great. I think you guys had been there about a couple of years back. Your mother and father must be eagerly waiting to see their grandson who has grown so big now."

Rahul's mother appeared to be sad when she said, "But you are going to spoil our Holi by being absent. I will miss you. My Holi would be colorless without you. Tell your father-in-law, that he has given his daughter to me rather than me giving my son to him."

Rahul laughed and said, "Your favorite son is with you. Don't worry about Holi. I have spent most of the Holi vacations with you. I promise to celebrate next year's Holi with you."

Rakesh took a bite from the cookie and said, "Ankita, I just fail to understand this. How could you get this stubborn guy to agree to go for a journey?"

Ankita was going to take a sip but stopped her cup midway and said, "You are right, he says that he falls sick at the sight of a train."

Rakesh laughed and said, "In fact, he used to be frightened by train when he was a child. My mother is a witness. Once we were waiting for a train at Samastipur station. He was about nine years old and I was about fourteen. Do you know what happened? The moment he saw the huge steam engine coming towards him, he panicked and peed in his pants."

Rahul was feeling embarrassed and said, "I was just a small kid at that time."

Everybody had a hearty laugh. But Rakesh had not had enough of it. He called the kids and explained that whole story to them. The kids too laughed at seeing Rahul's face.

While they were talking, Poonam and Ankita were going through the elaborate process of making biryani. Poonam took out long grain Basmati rice; kept for some special occasions. She marinated the chicken with curd and many kinds of spices. Pressure cooker replaced the handi which is generally used for making biryanis. Nevertheless, the heady aroma coming from the pressure cooker was an indication of the delicious food which was going to be served.

Rahul took a long breath in order to fill his olfactory senses with the nice aroma. He said to Poonam, "Bhabhi, switch off the exhaust fan otherwise this aroma would awaken your neighbors. They would form a queue outside your door to demand biryani."

Hearing that, Poonam laughed out loudly.

All of them were served piping hot biryani. Raita was served as a side dish. Because of a greater number of people, the food was served on the carpet. The carpet was duly covered with newspaper to prevent any spillage damaging the carpet. Antara was helping her mother in arranging plates and bowls. Aryan and Samaksh arranged the glasses. Then biryani was served on a big platter so that everyone could help himself/herself.

While they were enjoying the dinner, Rakesh asked, "You will have to book the tickets in advance. You are planning to travel on which date?"

Rahul was tearing on a soft and succulent piece of chicken. He replied, "I think, we will start on the first of March. Hope to find tickets for that date because it would be too early for the real Holi rush to begin. "

Rakesh said, "Hmm! You are right. But you never know the website of railways. It behaves in strange ways the moment you are in dire need of a ticket."

Rahul said, "Yeah, I know. But I am confident of my typing skills and of the ease at which I navigate through internet."

"You are talking as if you were a software engineer; writing codes all through your life" saying that, Rakesh raised both his hands and moved them as if they were moving on some imaginary keyboard.

Rahul said, "You are forgetting that I must have booked your tickets many a times in the past."

Rakesh said, "But you have never booked a ticket for the festival season. I hope, you don't miss getting a ticket."

Rahul then replied, "Ok, I will call you for help on first January, when I will attempt to book a ticket. Is it fine with you?"

By the time they finished their dinner and discussions it was eleven pm. Rahul then took his brother's permission and went back to his home. Ankita and Aryan were quietly following him. They were feeling sleepy after a heavy meal and endless discussions. It was a perfect end to a perfect day. The day started with the plan for the Holi vacations; which was perfectly accompanied by a sumptuous breakfast. It ended with delicious biryani and a good time with the whole family.

4

Booking the ticket

After about one and a half week, the old year ended; paving the way for the New Year. It was first of January; the New Year Day. This was the day when Rahul needed to book the tickets in advance. Seeing Rahul getting up from the bed quite early, Ankita wondered, "Why so much hurry? Are you going to buy some flowers for me to wish me a Happy New Year?"

Rahul said with a grin, "No, I am going to buy train tickets for you to wish you a Happy New Year."

Ankita appeared to be pleased when she said, "It sounds good that we are going to travel much earlier than Holi. This may ensure us a confirmed ticket."

Taking out a bottle of water from the kitchen, Rahul said, "I was thinking on the same line. Holi is on the sixth of March. We will book a ticket for the first March. Hope, we will get confirmed tickets and will not to have to face too much crowd while boarding the train. There is always a risk of stampede at railway station during the festival season."

Hearing that, Ankita said, "Have not you heard the news of stampede at New Delhi railway station which happened during last year's rush during Chhath vacations? I sometimes feel ashamed that such stampedes always happen when the people of Bihar create a ruckus on the platform."

Rahul replied, "You are right. This gives such a bad name to the Biharis. People get a perception that all the Biharis are like this only; the dumb-heads."

Ankita asked, "By the way, we are going to travel by which class?"

Rahul appeared to be surprised by that question. He replied, "Why? We are going to travel by third AC. Don't worry about traveling by sleeper class."

Ankita appeared to be worried, "But AC tickets are costly. Do you think we are in a position to afford AC tickets? We have to manage for capitation fees for Aryan's admission in some reputed school."

Rahul appeared to be talking like a professor when he said, "Traveling by sleeper class can be unsafe; especially during the festival rush. So many people with general tickets tend to enter the sleeper class. The problem worsens during the festival season. You never know when someone gets away with your luggage and valuables. AC compartments are much safer. Their doors are usually locked during the journey. Very few unauthorized persons enter the AC compartments. We can spend some extra money for buying some sort of insurance against any untoward incident."

After that, Rahul raised his face to look towards the ceiling and raised his right hand in air while he was saying, "Moreover, we travel once in a blue moon. So, spending some extra money can always be justified."

The bookings start at 8:00 AM. Rahul switched on the computer and router well in advance. Ankita and Aryan pulled a couple of chairs near Rahul's chair. They were sitting besides; with heavy sense of anticipation.

Meanwhile, the doorbell rang. It was Rahul's brother; Rakesh. He had come to help Rahul while booking the ticket. Then Aryan's Nana made a call on Rahul's phone. He said, "Hope you remember that you need to book a ticket today? Try to be lightning fast while filling the names and other details on the railways website. All the available tickets are booked in a flash."

One of Aryan's Mama owns a travel agency in Patna. His name is Pankaj. Now, he was on the line. He called to give his expert advice. Rahul dreads talking to Pankaj because 90% of his talks are about beating around the bush. He seldom comes to the point while talking on phone. Aryan's Mama continued his talkathon for about 10 minutes. Most of the talks he made hardly made sense but finally he told, "You must be very swift otherwise the railway's ticket booking portal would begin to show REGRET in no time."

Rahul asked, "Why don't you do me a favor? You are an expert at booking train tickets. Can you book a ticket for us?"

Aryan's Mama replied, "I would have happily done this for my only Jija. Bu you know, this is the peak season for my business. I don't want to lose my customers. I too need to keep my kitchen hearth warm. You are internet savvy. You can easily do this. I am confident about you. My father had found a prodigy in you while searching a suitable match for my sister."

Rahul just laughed and disconnected his phone. Rahul logged in on the IRCTC website at 7:55 AM sharp because he did not want to leave anything to chance. The familiar webpage with light blue color scheme came on the screen.

The logo of IRCTC was on the top left corner and the sign in box displayed in the middle of the screen. He could notice that the website had begun to ask for CAPTCHA while signing in.

Rahul was flabbergasted. He mumbled, "What is the use of CAPTCHA? I always find them highly annoying. Search Google and you will find a very long and highly technical expanded form of CAPTCHA which says, "Completely Automated Public Turing test to tell Computers and Humans Apart". A CAPTCHA or OTP (One Time Password) appears to be very good when financial transactions are involved but what is the use of CAPTCHA just for logging in to a website to book a train ticket."

Rakesh was sitting on a chair just behind Rahul's chair. He said, "At this juncture, we cannot afford to argue about the futility of CAPTCHA. There is no other way than to follow the dictum of the railways."

Rakesh continued, "Now, you have succeeded in signing in. Select the starting station from the dropdown list. Now, select the destination from the dropdown list below that. Select the date of journey, and select e-ticket."

In fact, you get two options while booking a train ticket online. One of the options says i-ticket and another option says e-ticket. The 'i-ticket' is the ticket in physical form; similar to what you get while booking a ticket from the booking counter at any railway station. It is delivered at your doorstep by courier. The e-ticket is in soft copy. You can take a printout to show it to the ticket checker during the journey. Alternately, you can also carry the soft copy in your smartphone or laptop. Even showing the text message from your mobile phone is enough for the ticket checker.

Rahul replied, "Done. Oh no! The next page is taking too much time to open. Let us pray."

Rakesh was almost leaning over Rahul's head. He said, "Yeah, I can see the small circle moving endlessly; showing it is still searching the webpage." Both of them could hear each other's pulse.

Rahul was worried now, "My watch is already showing 7:59. We cannot do anything if the page opens even a couple of minutes after eight."

Rakesh almost shouted in joy, "Great! The next page has finally loaded. Hurry up now. Select the train."

Rahul selected the train Freedom Fighter and said, "This train has more number of AC coaches so chances of getting a confirmed ticket are on a higher side."

Rakesh said, "Good decision. Now, fill the name of passengers and other details. Do you have your net banking details ready in front of you?"

Rahul was typing furiously. He indicated towards a sticky pad and said, "Yeah, I have written the user ID and password for net banking on this sheet of paper. I don't want to take chance."

Rakesh said, "Ok, enter your mobile number. ………...Now, you will have to type another CAPTCHA. ………Good! ……...Now click on the 'Pay Now' button."

After filling all the required details, Rahul finally clicked on the 'Pay Now' button. Till now, everything was working at good speed. Once he clicked on the 'Pay Now' option, another page opened which asked for the name of the bank. Rahul selected his bank's name from the drop down list. The next click redirected the webpage to the bank's website.

After filling the user ID and password, Rahul clicked on the final 'Submit' button. A message flashed on the screen telling that a certain amount had been deducted from Rahul's bank account. Within a few seconds, he also got a text message from his bank about the deduction of money from his account. But they were still waiting for the webpage to redirect to the railways' website.

Everybody was silent; staring at the computer screen. Their faces were full of anticipation and many other emotions. Rahul was fiddling with a ball pen, while Rakesh was continuously tapping the back of a chair with his fingers. Ankita and Aryan had their mouths open as if their lower jaws were going to touch the floor. Out of all the emotions, the sign of worry was more prominent. After what seemed an endless period of waiting, they could finally see the webpage of the railways. The ticket was booked but it showed that all the tickets were under waiting list. Now, everyone's face was showing a single emotion, i.e. of deep anguish and frustration.

Rahul, Ankita and Aryan sat for a while with long faces. Rakesh was trying to console them, "Don't worry. One of my friends is a high level officer in the railways. I will talk to him. I am sure he will help us in getting your tickets confirmed."

Rahul raised his eyebrows and replied, "It sounds good. Please talk to him as early as possible. I am also thinking of giving it another try tomorrow morning."

Ankita said, "And siphon all your bank balance to the Indian Railways. Do you know? How much time they take while returning the money to your bank account?"

Rahul looked at Ankita and said, "Yeah, I know. Sometimes, it takes more than a week to get your money back."

While they were doing the post mortem of their failed endeavor, Aryan's Mama from Patna came on the phone line. He asked, "What happened? Did you find success in booking confirmed tickets?

Rahul replied, "No! We failed. What to do now?"

Hearing that, Pankaj said, "Don't worry. All these waiting lists are inflated ones. You will get confirmed births just a day before the date of journey. In fact, there is a deep nexus between railway officials and touts. The cut from a travel agent's commission goes to grease many palms. But if you don't get confirmed births, you can always cancel your tickets."

Rahul asked, "Cancel my tickets and earn the wrath of your sister! I am getting a really friendly advice from my dear brother-in-law. Can you help us in getting these tickets confirmed?"

Pankaj said, "Ha! Ha! I am sorry, but I am not in a position to help you in getting these tickets confirmed. The rates are very high due to the festival rush. It will not look proper for me to ask for some extra money from you guys for getting confirmed tickets."

Rahul said, "Then why the hell are you in the business of travel agency? Sometimes, you should think above your commercial interest."

Pankaj said, "Calm down. I am nothing but a small fry in this business. After cancelling your ticket, you still have chance to book 'Tatkal' tickets. Now-a-days, the government has even announced a 'Premium Tatkal' scheme. You get to see dynamic pricing under this scheme; on the line of flight tickets. That will be very costly but you only get a confirmed ticket under this scheme. No waitlist, no RAC. Sounds great, isn't it."

Rahul said, "But I am sure, the railway only shows premium class while charging excess money for the same ticket. There is nothing premium in the facilities. You get the same births in the same train. You get to eat similarly horrible meal which is being served by the IRCTC. Moreover, there is no guarantee of reaching your destination on time even if you pay a premium on fare. Now, instead of the numerous touts, it is the railway which is doing black-marketing of tickets."

Pankaj said, "We are common people. We cannot change this system. We have no other way than to bear with it."

After about a week; Rahul was once again on his mission to book tickets, this time he needed to book the return tickets. He thanked the almighty and the railways because booking confirmed tickets never appeared so easy. He took the return tickets for 10th March. As he did not want to take chances, so he booked the return tickets from Patna, that too by Rajdhani Express.

After booking the tickets, life appeared to come to the mundane ways but most of the experts in the family and neighborhood never allowed it to become normal. Everybody was coming up with all sorts of theories regarding the prevalent black marketing of rail tickets.

Next day, Rahul met his neighbor, Mr. Khanna while walking in the park. Hearing his story, Mr. Khanna said, "Now-a-days, it is impossible to book a ticket without the help of a travel agent. These scrupulous railway staffs just manipulate the data to show waiting lists in almost all the trains."

Rahul said, "You are right. In fact, the website is made by human beings and any web administrator with proper rights can always play with figures."

Another neighbor; Mr. Pandey said, "One of my relatives is a travel agent. He has earned filthy amount of money from this business. Recently, he bought a duplex villa in the heart of Noida. Can you believe it? He was a non-entity just four years ago."

Mr. Khanna said, "One of my friends is working as a booking clerk in the Indian Railways. He gets to earn extra money during festival season. He says that he needs to share the loot up to the top level in the department. Haven't you noticed that many top politicians vie for the post of the rail minister? They consider the railways as the hen which lays golden eggs."

Rahul had also observed that the railway website begins to behave in a strange way whenever the bookings for a particular date open. By the time it comes to normal; all you get is the wait list or regret notice. Most of the newspapers, magazines, politicians and people usually boast about the largest pool of software professionals in India. Some people also claim that 30% of the employees at Microsoft are Indians. But it is beyond comprehension that why the railways cannot make a user-friendly website through which people could easily book tickets. Some people say that the website of the railways gets a heavy load of traffic and hence does not work properly during peak hours. I am sure it does not get more visitors than Google or Facebook. If they are unable to do this, they can at least outsource the business of making and managing the website to some giant of the dot com. But that would hurt the pride of the nationalist brigade and would give a chance to many new guardians of the pride of the country to come into existence.

Right from the 25th February, Rahul started looking for the latest status of tickets. The waiting list number had begun to go down but it was doing so at snail's pace.

As the date of journey was coming near, Rakesh called his friend who was working for the railways. Rakesh told him, "Hey, Jivendra, it is me. In fact, I have called you for a help. Rahul; my younger brother; is planning to travel to Darbhanga for Holi vacations. Can you help him in getting his waitlisted tickets confirmed?"

Jivendra replied, "Oh, it is you. After a long time! How is Rahul? …….. In fact, now-a-days, I am posted at Lucknow. Had I been posted at New Delhi, I could have easily helped you. Sitting in the Ministry has its own benefits. But nobody listens to a person who is sitting away from the headquarters. I cannot assure you but I will give it a try. Hope you will not mind."

Rakesh told the PNR number to Jivendra; in the hope of getting some help.

Finally, on the morning of 28th February; the waiting list came down to 6, 7 and 8. Rahul knew it was the time to worry. Looking at his face, Ankita asked, "You appear to be worried. But you should be happy at not getting a confirmed ticket because it will help you avoid the torture of a train journey."

Rahul said, "I am least interested in traveling but I have to take care of my wife's and my son's interest too. You must have noticed the extreme joy on his face when Aryan got to know about our plan for Holi vacations. I don't want to rob him off this golden opportunity. After a couple of years, he will be in high school. Then he would seldom get a chance to enjoy his life. He will be too occupied in his studies."

Ankita said, "So, what are you going to do? Are you going to book a flight for Patna? No way, I am not going to allow this. This will put too much drain on our bank balance."

In fact, the system of tatkal ticket was introduced to help those passengers who make last minute plans for travel. Many people who travel for business purposes and people who have to face some sort of emergency formed the target group for tatkal ticket. But the caucus of travel agents and railway officials has turned tatkal into a farce. The booking window for next day's tatkal opens at 10:00 AM sharp and all the tickets get booked within a flash. Almost every major train has about 150 to 200 births under tatkal quota; if you include tickets of all the available classes. Looking at the huge number of trains in a huge country like India; there must be at least a million births under tatkal quota. But for normal people; like Rahul it is almost impossible to book a tatkal ticket. The government has made many rules to prevent unscrupulous bookings but the touts always find their way out of those rules. For example; you need to furnish a copy of an ID proof of at least one passenger to book the ticket. But fraudsters have become computer savvy and can easily forge documents using image editing tools. The huge gap in demand and supply could be the main reason for the prevalent black-marketing of rail tickets.

Once again, Rahul sat in front of his computer and logged in to railway website. He began clicking furiously on various options when the clock showed 10:00 AM. But the railway website refused to cooperate. It either gave error message or it was taking very long to open a particular page. By the time, the website resumed its normal behavior, the website was showing that all 'tatkal quota' was filled and one could only buy waitlisted ticket. Rahul remembered that Aryan's mama had told him that railways had introduced premium tatkal tickets some time back. And they only give confirmed tickets through premium tatkal. But there was a catch. They follow dynamic pricing for premium tatkal. This means that price goes on increasing with each subsequent booking; the way it happens in case of flight tickets. Many politicians go on harping on grand plans about how they are going to transform India into a developed country on the lines of western countries. While introducing the premium tatkal system, a politician said that the same system was in place in the UK. If you cannot make the world-class facilities in the train; you can at least introduce dynamic pricing of tickets so that people would get a feel of living in a developed country. However, in spite of paying a hefty premium you still get to travel in shoddy train compartments and in trains which are always running behind their schedules. Some people also rue the fact that it is now the railway which is indulging in black-marketing of tickets; in the name of dynamic pricing. People are also cooperative because it is better to pay in advance than haggling with the TTE (Travelling Ticket Examiners) in the train. At least you buy peace of mind by paying a premium and you are free from the possible insult meted out by the ticket checkers in the train.

Nevertheless, Rahul tried for premium tatkal and was at last successful in getting three confirmed tickets. But his heart sank when he saw the huge amount of money which was deducted from his bank account. The total price which he paid was more than thrice the price of normal ticket. So, it was a mixed feeling for Rahul. He was relieved to get confirmed tickets but was not happy about the price he was forced to pay for tickets.

On seeing Rahul's expressions, Ankita said, "What was the need for spending so much money? We could have cancelled the trip."

Rahul said, "I did not want to take risk of being targeted to your constant barbs. I had no other way but to pay the premium for these tickets."

Ankita said, "But this will make our whole plan awry. I was planning to buy new clothes for my parents and for my brothers."

Rahul said, "We can always do away with some old traditions. Even your parents would understand our problem."

Ankita said, "But it does not look nice. We are visiting my parents after a long gap. Have you seen that they come with new clothes for us whenever they visit us?"

Rahul said, "You are his only daughter and I am his only son-in-law. Your father has no more worry of arranging a marriage of a daughter. His two sons are ready for the marriage market and I am sure he is not going to leave that opportunity to extract the maximum possible amount from the bride's family."

Ankita did not appear to be pleased. She said, "Don't talk such nonsense about my father."

While they were talking, a phone call came from Aryan's mama. It was Pankaj on the line. Hearing about the premium tatkal tickets, he said, "You should have booked a flight ticket for the same price. You missed an opportunity to fly. At least my sister would have been happy. She has never travelled by a plane."

Rahul irritatingly said, "And who is going to pay for the taxi fare from Patna to Darbhanga? I know that I am talking to a big miser."

Pankaj laughed in reply, "But I am younger than you. It won't look good if I will pay for your taxi fare."

Rahul said, "I know you. You know how to talk your way out of a tricky situation. No problem, the price I have paid shows the value of my journey. After all, I am going to spend the Holi vacations at my in-law's place."

When Rakesh heard this news, he said, "Congratulations on getting confirmed tickets. But you must have paid through your noses. This shows the value you accord to your in-laws. Anyway, if you need some monetary help you can always tell me."

Rahul replied, "It is all right. At present I don't need extra money. I will tell you in case of need. Don't worry about that."

Aryan's Nana also called to congratulate Rahul and said, "It is good that you got success in getting confirmed tickets. But it is sad that you were forced to spend so much money on that. I am ready to reimburse for your ticket; if you wish."

Rahul said, "You are not my employer so you are not bound to do reimbursements. It won't look nice to take money from you."

5

Going to the railway station

About two months passed from the time when Bujhaavan and his friends had booked their tickets. It was the last week of February. They had planned to purchase many things for their families. Bujhaavan suggested, "Let us go to the Shani Bazaar (Saturday Market) for shopping."

Narayan asked, "It would be better if we go to the Lajpat Nagar or Sarojini Nagar market. We can get really nice dresses for our wives and children."

Ramchander gave a light pat on his back and said, "Look at this man. He is talking like a typical Delhi boy; wants to take a stroll in a fashionable market."

Hearing that, Bujhaavan said, "We cannot afford to do shopping at the Lajpat Nagar market. That would be too costly for us. The Shani Bazaar suits our budget. You can get things at cheaper rates at the Shani Bazaar."

Delhi is probably among some rare cities where the old tradition of weekly markets is still being maintained. Different localities get to witness weekly markets on different days of the week. At some places, it can be on

Monday, at others it can be on Tuesdays, Wednesdays and so on. Such markets are thronged by sellers who specialize in doing business in such markets. They set up their shops by late afternoon. Folding tables, plastic sheets and iron poles are supplied by the tent-houses for the purpose of creating makeshift shops. Rechargeable lights are supplied by enterprising entrepreneurs. At some places, the weekly markets can be on a grand scale. You can find almost any household item. People from the middle class usually visit such markets to buy fresh vegetables at cheaper rates. People from the lower classes visit such markets to buy many other things; ranging from utensils, buckets, mugs, ropes, clothes, bed-sheets, makeup kits, carry-bags, toys, suitcases, etc. You will also find many food-carts which sell street food in these markets. One can get most of the household items at much cheaper rates than in any conventional market. This is probably because of the low overhead costs involved in doing business in such markets. The retailer does not have to think about high rentals for the space. There is no need to maintain a warehouse, hiring sales staffs, paying electricity bills, etc. The good crowd of buyers and sellers create the old world charm of any weekly market which can often be seen in rural parts of

India. The ambience at such markets resembles that of a fair.

Bujhaavan and his friends went to the Shani Bazaar as per their plan. The market is organized in an empty ground which is surrounded by a boundary wall. A huge iron gate serves as the entrance to the market. Many vendors had parked their pushcarts near the entrance; on the footpath. The human mass from the market was overflowing up to the road; creating traffic bottlenecks for the peak-hour traffic. While Bujhaavan and his friends were entering through the gate they had to squeeze their bodies through the crowd. After entering the market, they could see rows of shops which were selling toys, pirated CDs, fruits, pickles and undergarments. This was followed by rows of shops which were selling dresses, bed-sheets, slippers, shoes, etc. The vegetable sellers were at the far end of the market. Rows of colorful lights added sparkle to the charm of the market. But the shopkeepers had left little space for smooth movement of customers. To make matters worse, some vendors had blocked the passage with their shops on bicycle. They were selling kachauri and sabji. Many people could be seen enjoying those kachauris.

Bujhaavan and his friends bought dresses for their wives and children. They also bought suitcases to carry those dresses. Narayan even bought a mixer grinder of some local brand. They also purchased some toys for their children. Bujhaavan purchased a tricycle for his son.

Once they were back from the bazaar, they began packing their luggage. By the time they finished the packing, it was apparent that they would have to carry too many heavy bags and suitcases. Narayan said, "It appears that we will have to hire a coolie for carrying these bags."

Jitan laughed and said, "All my life I have been carrying so much burden that I cannot even imagine hiring a coolie."

Bujhaavan said, "We have enough practice of carrying heavy loads on our head throughout the day. What is the point of wasting our money on the coolie? Hiring a coolie befits a rich person only."

Ramchander said, "Bujhaavan Bhaiya is correct. We are strong enough to carry our burden. You have not become a Tata or Birla so try to be within your limits."

Finally, their wait was over as it was the first of the March; the date of their journey. It was raining since morning. In spite of the heavy rains they went for work as they could not afford to lose on a day's earnings. All of them were back from work somewhat earlier than usual. They came back at about five in the evening. Bujhaavan said, "How are we going to reach New Delhi railway station?"

Narayan said, "We are not lucky enough to have a metro station nearby. I am not sure about the bus route."

Ramchander said, "I only know the bus route which goes to Kapashera; the place where I usually go for work."

Jitan said, "No bus driver will allow you with so much of luggage. We need to hire an auto-rickshaw."

Bujhaavan said, "Four people can easily sit in an auto-rickshaw, but what about our bags and suitcases. We will need to hire at least two auto-rickshaws. I think we need to hire a taxi. A taxi will be cheaper than two auto-rickshaws."

Jitan said, "Yes, you are right. Let us go to the Gupta Stationery. I have heard that he is also in the business of taxis."

They reached Gupta Stationery which was selling stationery items. The shop was well lit from outside as well as from inside. Beautiful stuffed toys were prominently displayed in glass cases. The whiff of cool air from the AC made them feel as if they had entered some lifestyle shop. Bujhaavan and his friends were awestruck when they saw thousands of pens on the racks. He asked the owner of that shop, "Sir, we need a taxi to go to New Delhi railway station. What are the charges?"

The shop owner said, "We charge one thousand rupees for dropping any passenger to New Delhi station. But we don't allow more than four people in a taxi."

Bujhaavan said, "We are just four guys but we have too many bags and suitcases."

The shop owner said, "Some of your bags can fit inside the boot. Some heavy items can be put on the rooftop rack. Don't worry about the luggage. When do you need a taxi?"

Jitan said, "Our train is at eight so we need to start right now."

Within about fifteen minutes, a white hatchback came to stop near the gate of their slum. They loaded their bags and suitcases in the boot and on the rooftop rack. The presence of CNG cylinder inside the boot did not leave much space for luggage. But the rack on the roof compensated for that. Some of the bags needed to be kept on their laps. They started towards the railway station at about six in the evening. Once the taxi crossed the Palam flyover, it was floating on the road because most of the traffic was on the opposite lane. But once they were headed towards Dhaula Kuan, the car's speed matched with that of a turtle. It was the typical peak hour traffic. Cars were caressing each other's bumpers. But many bikers were trying to make zigzag moves while trying to beat the traffic. Heavy traffic gave enough time to Bujhaavan and his friends that they could have clear picture of the maze of flyovers at Dhaula Kuan. Narayan muttered, "I fail to understand how these drivers remember the correct road out of this puzzle."

Dhaula Kuan is a major traffic junction where traffic from many major routes converges. Many flyovers and underpasses have been built to facilitate smooth flow of traffic.

The Airport Express line of the Delhi Metro also crosses through Dhaula Kuan. Bujhaavan and his friends could see an Airport Express train zooming past through the overhead line. Ramchander commented, "It looks like the trains from any foreign country; the trains which we usually see in posters."

Bujhaavan asked the taxi driver "Is this train allowed only for those who are going by flight?"

The taxi driver replied, "No. Anybody can buy a ticket and enjoy a ride."

Jitan could not conceal his glee and said, "It sounds good. We will go for a ride in this train once we return from our village."

The taxi driver said, "You can board this train at New Delhi and get down at Sector 22."

Jitan said, "We can do this on the day when we will be back from our village."

By the time they were through the traffic bottleneck at Dhaula Kuan, it was already seven. Bujhaavan looked at the time on his mobile phone and said, "Bhaiya, can you make it faster. Our train is at eight."

The taxi driver said, "I am trying but it is of no use. Most of the traffic lights are not working because of the heavy rain. This is the bane of our country. The moment it rains, almost all the traffic lights go out of order. I don't know what they do after producing so many engineers."

Narayan said, "You are right. There are many engineers in the area where I live. All of them are still studying in some coaching institute even after completing their course."

The taxi driver took a turn towards Chanakyapuri; which can be considered as the gateway to the Lutyen's Zone of Delhi. Wide roads with plenty of greenery on both sides could be seen. Many palatial houses and bungalow dotted the landscape. Almost all the embassies are present along this road; which was evident from flags of different countries fluttering atop different buildings. The taxi was now flying; literally. None of the drivers ever appeared to break the traffic rules. When people drive through the roads of Lutyen's Zone, they usually obey the traffic rules. It can be because of the ambience of orderliness; created by wide avenues, greenery and houses of all the topnotch ministers. It can be because of the fear of getting caught and punished while breaking the rules in this zone.

They looked at the Teen Murti with a sense of awe. They almost jumped in joy when they crossed the Saat Murti. Most of the roundabouts showed installations of busts and statues of various luminaries related to the freedom movement of India. After passing through numerous roundabouts, their taxi reached Connaught Place; the famous landmark of central Delhi. Bujhaavan said to Narayan, "Hey Narayan! Look at that tall flag-post. I have heard that it is the tallest flag-post in India."

Narayan popped out his eyes in wonder and said, "It is really huge. At least a hundred people must be needed to hoist that huge flag so high in the sky."

The taxi driver said; with some sense of authority, "They use a machine for the purpose. I have not seen but it hardly takes ten minutes to hoist the flag so high in the sky."

The taxi driver further said, "You have to board a train to Bihar, if I am correct. Then I must drop you on the Ajmeri Gate side of the railway station."

Bujhaavan and his friend shouted in unison, "Yes!"

The taxi stopped at the taxi bay just in front of the entrance gate of the railway station. Bujhaavan and his friends got down from the taxi. They took out their luggage and paid the fare to the taxi driver. After that, Bujhaavan said, "Keep an eye on the luggage while I am going to check the position of the train."

Bujhaavan went to the enquiry counter. Being an illiterate person, he had no other way than to ask from the person manning the enquiry counter. There was a small crowd near the enquiry counter. He asked the person who was sitting at the enquiry counter, "Sir, what is the position of Freedom Fighter express?"

The person at the enquiry counter gesticulated towards a white board. Bujhaavan said, "Err! In fact, I cannot read or write. I am illiterate. Sir, will you be kind enough to tell for my benefit."

The person at the enquiry counter said rudely, "Your train is late. It will not leave Delhi station anytime before 12 in the night."

Bujhaavan went back to his friends and told them, "Our train is late. It is not going to depart anytime before 12. Let us go to the waiting area. Everybody will carry his luggage. Keep an eye on your luggage."

Each of them put two heavy a suitcase and a carton on his head and was carrying another bag on his shoulder. Bujhaavan was carrying an additional bag and the tricycle. He suspended his bag from the left shoulder and the tricycle from the right shoulder. He had tied the tricycle with at thick rope for the purpose. They reached the scanner for security check. Looking at them, the police personnel asked them to open their bags. All of them opened their suitcases and bags. The policeman thoroughly checked each bag. While he was doing so, he was also hurling choicest swear words at them and was calling all sorts of name. The most annoying word he was using for them was 'Bihari'.

It is quite normal to call a person from Bihar as a Bihari. It is same as calling a person from Bengal as Bengali. But most of the people use the term 'Bihari' as a derogatory remark. It is often used for a person who may not be refined enough; from the perspective of the so-called 'elite' people.

The whole process must have taken at least twenty minutes. Finally, they could get the go ahead from the police. After that, they took the staircase to reach the first floor to go to the waiting area. After reaching the waiting area, they spotted a vacant corner and put their luggage. They kept their luggage at the centre and made a huddle around it. Bujhaavan; being the most experienced of the lot; said, "Be careful at this station. Keep an eye on our luggage. Don't talk to strangers. Try to show some confidence whenever a policeman comes to you. Only one person would go to toilet or to have food at a given time so that rest of us can keep an eye on our luggage. We will take turns to sleep so that our luggage is not left unguarded. I have given photocopy of the ticket to each of you so no need to worry. I am sure each of you is carrying your voter ID with you."

Narayan said, "But the travel agent had said that just one of the passengers ID is required while traveling."

Bujhaavan said, "But you never know the strange ways of railway staffs. They may use it as a pretext for extracting some money from us. It is better safe than to be sorry."

Thus, they began their endless wait for the train. After a while, Narayan took out a beedi to smoke. He was about to take out the matchbox when Bujhaavan said, "You will always remain an idiot. You should be aware that smoking is prohibited on railway stations. The police will fine five hundred rupees for that. "

Narayan innocently said, "But that person on the bench is smoking a cigarette."

Jitan said, "That person appears to be a literate and rich person. Any policeman would not dare to go near him. But looking at our faces anybody can easily tell that we are poor and illiterate. We can be easy targets for the police. Try to understand your limitations."

Narayan put back the matchbox and beedi in his pocket. Then he asked, "Can I take some tobacco to chew?"

Bujhaavan said, "Yeah, you can. Just prepare it for every one of us. We can always use the spittoon for that."

Narayan then took out a small plastic box. It was a white rectangular box with two chambers on opposite sides with a partition in between. The bigger chamber contained finely chopped tobacco while the smaller chamber contained slaked lime. He poured a handful of chopped tobacco on his left hand and took a pinch of lime. He used his right thumb to thoroughly mix the lime with tobacco; by rubbing his thumb against his left palm. After repeating the process for about five full minutes, the concoction was ready. Bujhaavan got the honor to be the first of taking his dose of chewing tobacco; followed by Jitan and Ramchander. Narayan; being the youngest of the lot; was the last to have his dose. They kept the chewing tobacco between the gum and the lower lip and began enjoying the essence of it. They were keeping mum; waiting for the nicotine to show its effect. After about two to three minutes each of them went to the spittoon; one by one; to empty their mouths which was full of nicotine mixed saliva. Then they felt a huge relief and began to discuss sundry topics.

Bujhaavan said, "I am fed up of this city. This city is so big that I fear being gobbled up by this city. I wish to settle in my village to spend a life of relative calm."

Jitan said, "But where is the work in our village? At least this city has given us some chance to earn money."

Ramchander said, "We get work only for six months at our village if we are lucky. But the landlord seldom makes the full payment. He always tries to blackmail us by his numerous loan offers. He had even confiscated my only goat when I failed to repay the debt."

Narayan said, "He is right. At least we get some semblance of dignity while working in this city. We also get paid on time and get work on most of the days of a month. Bujhaavan Bhaiya is getting old and hence is speaking like this."

While engrossed in their talks they did not notice that it was already half past nine. Suddenly, Bujhaavan looked at his watch and shouted, "Oh God! It is already half past nine. This is the time we need to think about our dinner. We can go in groups of two to have dinner from some eatery outside the station. Alternately, two of us can bring dinner for all of us. What do you say?"

Jitan said, "Let me go with Narayan to buy dinner for all of us. All of us will get a chance to enjoy our dinner together."

Narayan said, "If I am not wrong then Bujhaavan Bhaiya will take eight chapattis and Ramchander will take ten chapattis."

Bujhaavan said, "Yeah, you are correct. Take two plates of dal (pulses) and two plates of vegetable curry. Try to find some cheap looking eatery. Don't go for any fancy looking one."

Narayan and Jitan came on the main road outside the railway station premises. The sidewalk was occupied by makeshift shops which were selling various items; like snacks, mineral water, cigarette, pan masala, etc. Some buses were haphazardly parked on the road; blocking normal traffic. In spite of incessant honking from cars and auto-rickshaws, the bus drivers did not appear in a mood to give way. The auto-rickshaw drivers could somehow find their way to get out of that bottleneck. But car drivers did not have such luck. The huge façade of the multilevel parking was visible on the other side of the road. Looking at that, Narayan wondered, "What is this? Is it a mall? I never heard about a mall coming near railway station."

Jitan said, "Once an idiot, always an idiot. You need to go to a doctor to get your eyes checked. This is a car parking. They call it multilevel car parking. If you will try you can spot some cars even at the top level."

Narayan opened his eyes wide in wonder and said, "How do they take the car up to that height? Do they use some crane of elevator?"

Jitan said, "I don't know. We don't even need to know because we are not going to buy cars in our lifetime. Let a car owner figure this out. Why should we bother?"

Narayan said, "Yeah, right now we need to bother about finding cheap food."

After crossing the road, they went towards the bus depot which is towards the left. They could find some cheap looking eateries near the bus depot. It was somewhat dark around the bus depot so they were somewhat apprehensive. Jitan said, "Be careful and alert of any suspicious looking person. I don't want to be robbed off my money while looking to save money on food. "

Narayan said, "Let us hurry to buy whatever we can get in the name of food. There is no point in wasting time hearing the long menu from the waiter."

Jitan said, "All of them tell the same names of dishes; dal fry, mixed vegetables, paneer curry, shahi paneer, paneer butter masala, paneer korma, aloo dum, aloo butter masala, vegetable korma, tandoori roti, plain nan, butter nan, stuffed nan, plain rice, jeera rice, fried rice, vegetable fried rice, chicken fried rice, chicken curry, chicken masala, chicken korma, chicken butter masala, ……….."

They quickly bought chapattis, dal and some vegetable curry and rushed back to the place where their friends were waiting. They spread the newspaper in which all the chapattis were wrapped. They opened the polythene bags which contained dal and vegetable curry. So, the soiled newspaper served as their dinner plate and the polythene bags served as bowls for them. They found no problem in using their hands to enjoy the food because they have never felt the need for spoons or forks in their lifetime. Each of them was taking huge morsels. The dal and vegetable curry were dripping down from their wrists and elbows. Some of the curry was also dripping down from their lips. It was ghastly sight to say the least. After finishing their dinner, they were burping in unison. Narayan had to do the duty of cleaning up everything. He picked up the polythene bags and soiled newspaper to deposit them in the garbage bin. After that, they took turns to wash their hands and mouth at the wash basin in the public toilet. While doing so they must have sprayed lot of water all around; making the place even filthier.

After finishing the dinner, Bujhavan asked Narayan to make a fresh dose of chewing tobacco. Narayan duly obliged so that everyone could get the required kick from nicotine. Once their indulgence with tobacco was over, Bujhaavan went to the enquiry counter to know the latest update on their train's schedule. After coming back, Bujhaavan said, "He is telling that the train is further delayed. It is not going to arrive before three in the night. My watch is showing only half past ten. We have enough time to catch a few winks."

Jitan said, "You can enjoy the privilege of being the first person to enjoy a sleep because you are the eldest of the lot. I will wake you up after an hour."

Bujhaavan appeared to be pleased with that show of respect. He said like a real guardian, "It is ok. But be careful while I will be sleeping. If any ticket checker or any policeman tries to take you for a ride, just wake me up. I know how to deal with them."

Bujhaavan used a bag as pillow and slept on the floor. He was fast asleep within no time which was evident from his snoring. Rest of this team was keeping a watch on him and the luggage. When Narayan was caught napping after a while, he was ordered to make a fresh supply of chewing tobacco. People addicted to tobacco have a firm belief that it helps in fighting the urge to sleep. To avoid the overpowering urge to sleep, Jitan began narrating the stories from some Bhojpuri movies. Bhojpuri is a dialect which is spoken in eastern parts of UP and in western parts of Bihar. But Bhojpuri movies are quite popular throughout Bihar; especially among the rural and semi-urban people. Jitan was expert in mouthing many Bhojpuri dialogues which were double entendres. Ramchander and Narayan were playing the role of a captive audience for Jitan. Both of them were laughing at each dialogue from Jitan. While they were engrossed in that session, a policeman came near them and shouted, "Hey, you rustic fellows. What do you think of this place? Are you sitting at a toddy shop; enjoying your daily fix of the brew? What makes you think that laughing so loudly is allowed at a railway station? "

Narayan said with a child-like innocence, "Sir, we were just trying to enjoy while waiting for the train."

The policeman said with a wicked smile, "Have you come here to enjoy or to wait for the train? I can take you to jail for creating a ruckus at a public place."

Jitan said, "We are sorry sir. We will keep our mouth sealed from now onwards. We promise not to utter a single word. Please have some mercy on us. We are poor and rustic people."

The policeman hurled some choicest swear words at them and went away from there. While the policeman was walking away slowly, he was dragging his lathi (baton) on the floor and was creating an annoying sound. Jitan, Ramchander and Narayan were just looking at his silhouette which was growing fainter till it was out of their sight.

Once the policeman was nowhere in sight Ramchander said, "Nobody has respect for poor people. In fact, our faces and clothes easily give away our identity. Anybody then treats us like punching bags. We cannot enjoy a round of gossip even at a public place. We are nothing more than swine in this social setup."

Narayan said, "What is wrong in our clothes? I am wearing a new pair of jeans and a stylish T-shirt. The white sports shoes are further enhancing my style."

Nobody commented on that statement. Everybody was probably giving a silent consent to what Ramchander had just said.

Bujhaavan was woken up at about 12 in the night as it was time for Jitan to catch some sleep. Similarly, Ramchander and Narayan took their turns at sleeping according to their allotted timings. By four am, all of them were awake. Bujhaavan once again went to the enquiry counter only to find that the train was further delayed. But there was good news. The person at the enquiry counter told that the train would begin its journey at about eight in the morning. Hearing that, their faces lit up like hundred watt bulbs on that gloomy and cold night. Bujhaavan then said, "Let us go to the toilet to relieve ourselves. You will hardly get space in the train to do your daily chores. I am sure somebody would be occupying the toilet with his whole family and all the bags and luggage."

Narayan said, "What is wrong in that? Even I have spent my whole journey sitting in the toilet. There were many instances when I had to."

Ramchander said, "Yeah, I can understand. But it is not pleasant at all; with the nauseating smell pervading the air inside the toilet."

Bujhaavan said, "Don't waste your time in silly talks. The person with the strongest urge to go to the toilet can be the first person to go."

Hearing that, Jitan almost ran towards the toilet. He was followed by others with suitable intervals in between. Once they were through their morning ablutions, Bujhaavan said, "Keep looking for some tea-seller. There is nothing like a hot cup of tea in the early morning; especially during the cold season."

A tea-seller appeared in sight within a few minutes. He was shouting at the top of his voice to attract customers. Narayan called the tea-seller and asked, "Bhaiya, how much for a glass of tea?"

The tea-seller replied, "Ten rupees."

Jitan said, "It is too costly for a small glass of tea. Can you give us some discount as we are going to buy for four persons?"

The tea seller said, "I don't give discounts even if somebody asks for forty persons or even for four hundred persons. Don't waste my time. Just tell me if you really want it or not."

Narayan said, "Ok, give us four glasses of tea."

After taking the first sip, Bujhaavan said, "Hmm! This is called life. There is nothing like sipping hot tea in the waiting area of New Delhi railway station."

Jitan said, "You are claiming as if you are having tea in some glitzy looking restaurant at Connaught Place."

Bujhaavan said, "For people like us, this is nothing sort of a five-star hotel. There is no cost involved in imagination. All of us are entitled to enjoy this pleasure."

All of them were making strange noises while slurping the hot brew. Narayan even put his glass upside down over his mouth to enjoy the last drop of tea from the glass.

6

Rahul Goes to Railway Station

Finally, the D-day came when they had to board the train from New Delhi railway station. Rahul's brother; Rakesh; came early in the morning. He said to Ankita, "Don't bother about cooking for today. Poonam is cooking for all of you. For your convenience, we will bring the lunch here and all of us would enjoy the lunch together. She is also preparing food for you guys for the journey. This will give you plenty of free time to pack your bags."

Ankita said, "So nice of you. Homemade food is always good for a train journey. I don't like the idea of eating the food from the train pantry. The food is horrible. You need to shove it down your gullet."

Aryan jumped into conversation, "But I like their food tray with so many pockets for different items. Can you remember mom, once you bought a plate for me when we were coming from Patna?"

Ankita said to Aryan, "But nobody is going to eat those trays. Can you remember; how little food you ate from that plate. Almost all of the food was thrown in the garbage bin.

The chapatti was like a sheet of rubber. One needs very strong fingers and teeth to break those chapattis. In vegetable curry, you will get lots of watery curry with barely visible chunks of vegetable. The dal (pulse) contains more water than pulse. And the rice is of the worst quality."

Meanwhile, Rakesh said to Rahul, "I will drop you guys at the railway station by my car."

Rahul said, "But it is raining since last night. All the roads must have become puddles by now. It is risky to drive during rains. Your car may get stuck at the middle of the road if water enters the exhaust system."

Rakesh said, "Let us hope that the rain stops by noon. Then everything will be all right by evening."

Rahul said, "We don't have too many bags. We will manage by metro train. It will save time as well. No need to take so much pain for us."

Rakesh said, "It was an expected comment from a thoroughbred professional like you. Where is the question of taking pain when a person is going to drop his brother's family at the railway station?"

Rahul said, "Ok, you win. If the rain stops in time then we will go by your car."

It is an unwritten rule while someone goes on a journey. A male member from close circle is expected to accompany the passengers up to the railway station or bus stand. He needs to help the passengers in arranging the luggage inside the compartment. He is not expected to leave the platform until the train leaves the platform. All of you must have witnessed the familiar sight of waving hands whenever a train is leaving a platform. Many people get misty eyed while saying goodbye to the traveler. Many ladies start weeping, the moment a train is ready to depart. While some of the ladies weep inconsolably, many others stop when the person at the platform is no longer visible. Ladies have such a great ability to start weeping at short notice and to stop that too within a few seconds. It appears that they have some sort of instant switching mechanism in their tear glands.

While Ankita was busy packing her bags, Rahul and Rakesh were discussing various grand topics. They were having discussions on some really big issues; like the rising inflation in the country and the possible results of the presidential elections in the USA. Samaksh; Rakesh's son;

came with a jute bag, the kind we carry to the market. He took out some disposable plates and sandwiches from that bag and said, "Mummy has sent breakfast for everyone. Come and enjoy the piping hot sandwiches."

Samaksh and Aryan arranged disposable plates on the table. They put two pieces of sandwiches in each plate. Aryan took out a bottle of ketchup from refrigerator and poured ketchup in each plate. He poured copious amount of ketchup in his plate and in Samaksh's plate.

While eating the sandwich, Aryan said, "Umm! These are really tasty. I love potato sandwiches. This is really hot and spicy."

Rakesh said, "Do you know Ankita? The taste of sandwich could be even better had there been hot coffee to go along with it."

Ankita got the cue. She smiled and went to make coffee for everyone.

When Ankita was through with packing, she asked Rahul to have a look on the bags and baggage. There was a huge suitcase, two carry bags (made of nylon) and two jute bags. Looking at them, Rahul asked, "The suitcase must be full of your dresses only; leaving no space for my dress or Aryan's dress."

Ankita nodded her head in affirmative. Then Rahul said, "It appears that we are going for some marriage function in your family. Are you planning to change so many costumes during your stay in the village? It is a village, and nobody would be coming to see a catwalk. We should carry only as much luggage which can be easily carried by us; without hiring a porter."

Ankita said, "But I have seen you carrying even heavier luggage with aplomb. You are my he-man; all powerful."

Rahul said, "Don't try to inflate my ego. I am a simple man and not a super-man. Anyway, what do these two bags contain?"

Ankita replied, "One of the bags has your dresses and another has Aryan's dresses. The brown jute bag contains some bed-sheets, old newspaper, tissue paper and disposable plates and cups. The green one contains our slippers, lock & chain and paper soap."

Rahul opened the nylon bags and removed some of his and Aryan's clothes. After that, he was able to reduce one bag from his luggage. But Ankita did not appear to be pleased at his act.

After re-packing of bags, Rahul asked, "Have you kept Aryan's Identity Card from his school?"

Ankita asked, "Why? What is the need of an identity card? He is not going to participate in any painting competition."

Rahul said, "You can never predict the behavior of ticket checkers. They may doubt about his age; after looking at this overgrown boy. We may need to show his identity card to prove that he is still entitled to fifty percent discount on the fare by virtue of being less than twelve years of age."

Ankita took out Aryan's identity card at and kept it in the outermost pocket of the nylon bag.

Since Ankita finished packing her bags quite early so they decided to go to Rakesh's house to have lunch. The lunch was a simple fare. Poonam had prepared rice, dal and vegetable curry for lunch. After finishing the lunch, Ankita went on to help Poonam in making the food for the journey.

Poonam was busy preparing the food and snacks for the journey. Rahul asked, "What are you making for the journey?"

Poonam replied, "I am making litti for all of you."

Rahul said, "Sounds good. Litti is dry and hence easier to carry. Your fingers don't get spoiled while eating a litti. Just a couple of littis is enough to fill your stomach. The best part of carrying litti is carrying the taste of Bihar throughout your journey."

Litti is a popular delicacy from Bihar. Litti is like stuffed puri which is traditionally made in the shape of spherical balls and is baked on charcoal fire or on dung-cake fire. The stuffing is composed of roasted gram flour, garlic, green chilli and many spices. It is generally eaten with a mixture of mashed potato and brinjal and plenty of ghee (clarified butter). But Ankita will manage with tomato ketchup. This is the beauty of very high capacity of assimilation of Indians. Since ages, India has assimilated diverse cultures, costumes and cuisines. Ketchup can be found in most of the Indian households. It became popular with the masses only in the post-liberalization phase. Most of the modern Indian housewives may not know how to make the traditional tomato chutney and the blame easily goes to the all conspicuous tomato ketchup. Those of you who grew up during the period of Doordarshan may fondly remember the popular tagline from an advertisement of a popular ketchup brand which was, "It's different!"

Nobody likes the food which is being served by the caterer in train compartments. The food is highly priced and is of poor quality. One needs to shove that food down one's gullet. Even the vendors, who sell food items at platforms, do not know the basics of hygiene and quality. So, most of the people prefer to carry homemade food while going on a long journey by train. Even the so called mineral water sold in trains is of spurious quality. Most of the packets show brand names which appear and sound similar to leading brands but leading brands are rarely available.

While litti was being made, Rakesh said to Rahul, "Have you checked the status of the train which is arriving from Darabhanga? Do you know the same rake is sent back for the return journey? Until and unless the train from Darbhanga arrives on time your train is not going to leave Delhi on time."

Rahul logged on to the railways' website only to find that the train from Darbhanga was yet to reach New Delhi. The train was running eight hours behind its schedule. Rahul appeared to be worried, "The train is way behind its schedule. What will happen if the train would be cancelled? My wife will kill me."

Rakesh laughed and said, "Don't worry. They don't cancel trains during festival season. It will create a riot on the railway station."

Rahul said, "Our train is not going to reach New Delhi before ten in the night. Add another four hours at the washing pit, and the train is likely to leave Delhi not before 2:00 AM in the night."

Rakesh said, "Don't worry. I will drop you at the railway station no matter even if I need to drive during midnight."

Rahul said, "The rain is refusing to stop. What is the point of driving during night, that too when it is raining heavily? It can be risky. Although people of Delhi obey traffic rules most of the time, yet you get demons behind wheels during night. Have not you heard that most of the road accidents in Delhi happen during late night or early morning?"

Rahul further said, "I think it will be better to go by metro train. The metro station is at a walking distance from our home. We are not carrying too many bags with us. It will also help us in saving time and money. You need not suffer the avoidable harassment."

Rakesh said, "But the last metro rail departs at around 11 in the night. So, you will have to leave for the metro station by 10 pm. It will be better to reach the railway station and begin your endless wait for the train. The Indian Railways will never mend its ways."

Rahul said, "During my stint in the sales job, I had developed a habit for waiting for hours for trains. And I suffered a lot because of that. Once I must have waited for almost ten hours for my train at Gaya. People are also used to it. People don't consider a train late if it comes within half an hour of its schedule. This is a good example of typical Indian mindset. Do you know what happened when I was in the UK?"

Ankita said, "I think you had told that story earlier. But tell me what happened."

Rahul said, "One day, I was waiting at the York railway station to board a train for Leeds. About twenty people were also waiting for the same train. Then there was an announcement that the train would be delayed by five minutes. The announcement also said about an alternate train which was going to depart within the next five minutes from another platform. Hearing that announcement, all the people rushed to board that train. I was the single soul left on the platform; because a five minute delay was nothing for me. People were staring at me as if I had come from another planet."

Ankita said, "That is why they are developed country and we are still developing country."

After finishing the dinner, Rahul, Ankita and Aryan got ready for the journey. Rahul was wearing a pair of blue jeans, sweat-shirt and a jacket. He was also wearing a pair of sneakers from some reputed brand. Ankita was wearing salwar suit which was having white floral prints over a light blue background. She was donning a jacket over her kurta. She was also wearing sneakers. Aryan was wearing olive green shorts with white t-shirt and leather jacket. They locked their flat and began their trek to the metro station. There was a suitcase, one nylon-bag and two shopping bags which were made of jute. The suitcase was full of Ankita's belongings and had no room for others' items. In spite of Rahul's repeated warnings, the suitcase was packed to its full capacity and was really heavy for its size. Rahul's and Aryan's clothes easily fitted in the nylon bag. Carrying all the luggage down from the fourth floor flat was not an easy task for Rahul but he somehow managed it.

Rahul was furious after carrying the heavy suitcase downstairs. He fumed, "You will never change. We are not going there to attend a marriage. We will stay there for just a week and you have packed as if you are going for a whole month. Your father did not marry you to a coolie nor to a Superman. You also know that I don't like hiring a coolie. I will be huffing and puffing with the luggage, and you will be just taking a leisurely stroll on the platform. Nice idea for enjoying your journey."

Ankita just smiled but did not utter a single word. Aryan was also smiling at seeing Rahul's plight.

Rakesh was downstairs with his family. Rakesh, Poonam, Rakesh's mother, Antara and Samaksh had come to see them off. Rahul, Ankita and Aryan took the blessings of their elders by touching their feet. The ritual was repeated by Samaksh and Antara as well. Ankita hugged her mother in law and Poonam. Rakesh's mother felt a lump in her throat while she said, "Take care and enjoy your Holi. I will miss you."

Metro station was at walking distance from Rahul's house. After walking about 200 meter from their house, the wide road ended on a T-point. They took a left turn which led to a narrow street. Too much encroachment in the lane made it difficult to negotiate even for pedestrians. To make matters worse, the lane was full of potholes and pebbles. Puddles of water further compounded the problem. The lane resembled more of a bazaar than a residential area. Most of the people had rented out ground floor to shopkeepers, and tenant families lived on upper floors. There were all kinds of shops; like garment shop, grocery store, sweat meat shop, stationary store, eateries, etc. in the lane. There were two ATMs as well in the lane. All these developments were new as they happened once a metro station began operations in the area. Since it was night hence there was not much crowd in the lane. Most of the shops had already downed their shutters and only a few eateries were open and were doing brisk business. Even the stray dogs appeared to be lazy because of the cold night. The lane was well lit because of the recent installation of LEDs on streetlights; and thus it was a saving grace.

Rahul was walking ahead; carrying the heavy suitcase in one hand and the bag slung on the opposite shoulder. The load appeared too much for Rahul as he was of medium height. Ankita and Aryan were carrying one jute bag each. Although the suitcase had wheels in its base but given the condition of the lane, it was better to carry the suitcase just by lifting it. So, it was a familiar sight of a typical Indian family going on a journey. The husband carries most of the burden; with wife and children providing some minor support.

Finally, they emerged from the lane and came on the main road. The end of the lane had a row of shops; selling pan masala, cigarettes and candies. The food cart of Jan Aahar was already closed. The Jan Aahar scheme was launched with much fanfare by the government. The food carts of Jan Aahar use to sell basic food at subsidized rates. Once, Rahul had also bought that food and had appreciated the hygiene and taste of the food. The whole sidewalk was occupied by different kinds of vendors so Rahul and his family had to carefully make way through them. The main road was bustling with traffic. The entrance to metro station was choked because of many auto-rickshaws trying to jostle with each other in the hope of getting passengers. A huge backlit board displayed the name of the metro station. Newly planted saplings could be seen in neat rows; with brick cordon around them. A beggar was trying to sleep on the steps which led to the underground station. It was a perfect picture of many stark contrasts which we often encounter. The façade of the metro station was speaking of a modern India which is trying to leap in the future. Latest models of cars were zooming through the wide road; telling the story of a growing India. The beggars and auto-rickshaws were telling the dark reality which lies behind the gleaming façade.

Rahul and his family went down the stairs to reach a well lit atrium. On the right, there was a vending machine displaying all kinds of chocolate bars. On turning left, they entered a long corridor which led to the check in gate of the metro station. Two automatic ticket vending machines could be seen along the corridor; with bold display of 'OUT OF ORDER'. There were only a few people near the ticket counters. Rahul was carrying pre-paid cards so he did not need to buy tickets from the counter. Rahul and Aryan went to the entrance meant for male passengers, while Ankita went to the entrance for female passengers. The luggage was hurriedly put on the conveyor leading to the huge scanning machine. The security guard was staring blankly on the computer screen. He appeared to be disinterested and bored because of monotony of his work. Ankita disappeared behind the makeshift cubicle for security check. After passing through the security check, Rahul collected the bags and suitcase and rushed towards the turnstile.

Ankita was almost running behind him when one of the security guards called her and told, "Madam, you forgot to collect your handbag."

Ankita sheepishly smiled and rushed back to collect her handbag from the conveyor. Rahul heaved a sigh of relief and said, "Thanks God, your mistake has been discovered in time. Otherwise, you would have to manage in the train without your face-wash and nail-polish."

While standing near the turnstile, Aryan looked at the vast pathway ahead which was shining with diffused light. The gleam in his eyes was reflecting those lights. There was an elevator right in the middle of that pathway. The symbol of wheelchair on the elevator gate meant that it was meant for disabled persons. But some young people could be seen jostling to get inside the elevator. Aryan must have travelled by metro rail a number of times yet he always appears to be overawed by wonderful ambience of metro rail stations in Delhi. He was also watching some murals on the walls which displayed the rich cultural heritage of Delhi. The murals were full of clichés; like silhouette of the Red Fort, Qutab Minar and Lotus Temple as the predominant theme.

The turnstile swiveled once the prepaid card was swiped, and Rahul, Ankita and Aryan crossed the turnstile one by one. Rahul and his family took the staircase to go down to the platform. Finally, they reached the platform only to notice that the next train would arrive after 9 minutes. The huge display board overhead was showing the time for expected arrival of the next train. A whiff of fresh air was coming intermittently from the vents in the ceiling of the platform. Most of the people were standing in anticipation. But some people could be seen sitting on steel benches which were arranged in circular fashion around the huge pillars. While the train frequency is high during peak hours, it is very low during non-peak hours. There were not more than 20 passengers on the platform and most of them appeared to be headed towards the railway station to board some train. It was apparent from the luggage they were carrying. When the metro train arrived, most of its bogies were almost vacant. People could be seen enjoying the luxury of too much space in the compartment; which seldom happens during daytime. Aryan also got the luxury of doing an impromptu pole dance inside the coach. During peak hours, you should consider yourself lucky even if you get proper space to stand in the compartment. However, metro train has really made the life very easy for the common people of Delhi. A ride in taxi could have taken at least 45 minutes to reach railway station but it takes just a little over 20 minutes by metro train. You also get the cozy comfort of air-conditioned compartment sans all the dust and grime which is associated with going by a bus or auto-rickshaw. Many taxi operators ply air-conditioned taxis but the traffic snarls take out the joy of traveling by a car.

Once they were inside the metro train, the automatic doors of the compartment were shut and the train started catching speed. The stainless steel seats where gleaming against off white background of the compartment. Pre-recorded voice of announcers began to announce the name of the next station in Hindi and English. Male and female voices could be heard alternately. Everything was working in clockwork precision. Overhead display boards near each gate were displaying the names of different stations of the route. Green light was flashing against the name of the next station. The compartment was squeaky clean. This was in total contrast to the real world outside. The high level of cleanliness in metro shows that given proper facilities and effective deterrents, even Indians can be taught to stick to certain codes of conduct.

After about 20 minutes, the metro train reached New Delhi Metro Station; where Rahul and his family got down from the metro train. Carrying the luggage was much easier because of smooth surface of metro station platform. Presence of escalator made it much easier to carry the luggage upstairs. Finally, they came out of the metro exit gate to face the frenetic ambience of New Delhi railway station. Rahul could see the huge façade of New Delhi railway station in front of him. On the left side was the car parking which was full of rubbles and potholes. It was quite dark in the car parking as most of the lights were not working. Stench of urine added to the gloomy condition of the car parking. There were two huge banyan trees near the entrance to the parking. A small stall was present under one of the trees; selling pan masala, candies and cigarettes. The cafeteria near the entrance of the metro station was still open but only a few customers could be seen around it.

They needed to cross four lanes to reach the entrance of the railway station. The first two lanes were choked with taxis, cars and auto-rickshaws and it was really difficult to find a way through them. The third lane had some cycle rickshaws and the fourth lane was totally free for pedestrians. Entrance to foot-over-bridges could be seen on extreme left and extreme right sides of the main entrance to the railway station. It has been raining since morning so the weather was very cold even at the beginning of March. Cold wind was blowing with full ferocity which sent shivers down the spine. It was a typical 'Dilli ki sardi'; which has been immortalized in popular folklore and in numerous Bollywood songs. After passing through the security check, Rahul decided to go upstairs to find some space in the waiting area. His train was to leave from platform number 16 so they entered from Ajmeri Gate side of the railway station. Platform number 16 is nearest from this side. When Rahul enquired about the waiting room for A/C passengers, he came to know that it was on platform 1; near Paharganj side of the railway station. He was least interested in trudging with so much of luggage to reach platform 1 and so preferred to wait in the non-A/C waiting room which was on the first floor near the main entrance. The waiting room was full of people but Rahul could get three vacant seats on one of the benches. He asked Ankita to rush to occupy the seat before anyone else could do. They arranged the luggage neatly near the bench and began mentally preparing for the long hours of eventual but agonizing wait for the train.

7

The Long Wait

It was not a large waiting room; given the huge number of passengers who throng the New Delhi railway station every day. There were four rows of benches with each bench having a seating capacity for three persons. Two of the rows were with their backs to the walls and other couple of rows was in the middle with their backs towards each other. There were eight benches in each row. Thus there were thirty two benches; with a seating capacity for 108 people. The walls of the waiting room where painted in white; with white tiles up to the skirting of each wall. Clusters of tube lights could be seen on the ceiling; throwing diffused light on each group of benches. A huge wall clock and a speaker could be seen at one end of the waiting room. The clock was showing correct time; in 24 hour format which is the norm for railways timings. The speaker was covered with a thick coat of dark soot, and cobwebs provided further adornment to it. Announcements about trains were hardly audible probably because of the worse condition of the speaker or because of some other technical fault.

No sooner they sat on the bench, Rahul could sense a very powerful stench of urine coming from the toilets in the waiting room. The doors were left ajar and the toilets were in complete darkness. The stench was too much for them. Rahul could see that Ankita had already covered her nose with her dupatta (kind of scarf). He said, "This stench is unbearable. Let me go out and find some vacant seats in the open area. Keep an eye on the luggage."

Ankita said, "While coming upstairs, I saw the board for 'Executive Lounge'. I had heard about it on TV. Why don't you go and check the facilities?"

Rahul said, "That is giving five-star facilities to passengers with matching rates. I have seen their rates on railways' website. They are charging Rs. 300 per person for the first three hours. After that, it is Rs. 125 per person per hour. You will get free meal but you need to pay an extra amount of rupees one hundred seventy five if you want to take shower. Towel, soap and shampoo shall be provided to you. It is already half past eleven so no chance of getting the free meal. We need to wait here for at least ten hours. We will end up paying a huge amount just for enjoying the comforts of the premium facilities. That is not meant for people like us. That is for people who often travel by first class AC. I have already paid a hefty premium for tickets and am not in a position to dare to pay more for the waiting hall."

Rahul then went out to find some seat in the open area. The open area did not have stench and he could find a person who was occupying a whole bench and was trying to sleep on that. Rahul first requested that person to give seat but when polite language did not work, he was at his savage best to bring that person to his senses. Thus, they shifted themselves and their luggage to the open area to avoid the stench which was pervading inside the waiting room. Aryan started munching on potato chips to kill time. Ankita plugged earphones and tried to immerse herself in music. Rahul took out a magazine and tried to focus on latest news story.

Almost all the benches were full of people. Most of the people were trying to take a nap. The late hours and the cold weather probably had augmenting effect on the ambience. The area was almost silent which is uncharacteristic of any public place in India. During normal hours, the cacophony can be too much for your comfort. But in this case, people were probably too tired of agonizing wait or their senses were numbed due to cold weather. After the row of benches, Rahul could see many people sleeping on the floor. The person who was earlier sleeping on the bench was sitting besides Rahul. A horrible stench was coming from his socks. It appeared that he had not washed his socks since a long period. From his shabby dress, he appeared to be a casual laborer. When the stench became too unbearable for Rahul, he had to strongly ask the person to wear his shoes so that the stench could be minimized. Rahul was surprised that the person easily agreed to put on his shoes. But when he looked that he was still being stared by Rahul, he left the scene.

On a bench in front of Rahul, there was a middle-aged man. He was quite bulky right from tip to toe. He was wearing woolen trousers and faux leather jacket. His head was covered with a woolen cap and his face and ears were covered with a muffler. He was keeping his feet at the top of his luggage and was trying to doze off. Rahul could not understand but there was something strange about that man. It was probably his getup or the relative calm on his face; Rahul was unable to guess. Rahul could see some GRP (railway police) personnel making the round of the area. Within no time, one of the GRP personnel came near that person and began abusing him. The policeman was hurling choicest obscenities but the person was trying to maintain his calm.

The policeman asked, "Hey, it is you again. What do you think of the railway station? Is it your ancestral home you got as heritage? I have been watching you for the past four days. You appear to be a regular."

The person replied, "Actually, I have fallen in bad times. I am working as a sales representative for a small company in Daryaganj. The company does not pay me enough so I cannot afford to book a hotel room. They have called me to Delhi for discussing the falling sales."

The policeman said, "Go and discuss your problems with the owner of the company. Why are you squatting on the railways' property?"

The person replied, "Earlier I was in a good paying job. The moment I crossed forty, they kicked me out of the job. I have grown up children and I have to feed my family. I have been trying hard but unable to get a decent job. Believe me, I am not a criminal but a normal guy. I hope to go back to my town by tomorrow. Please allow me to sleep here at least for tonight."

The policeman hurled some more abuses at that person and then left the scene. After that, the person took out about half a dozen bananas from his bag and ate all of them as if he was in some hurry. While he was doing so, tear drops could be seen rolling down his eyes. Probably, eating the bananas was a way for him to console himself.

Aryan had finished a packet of chips and was looking all around to find a garbage bin. He asked Rahul, "Papa, can you see any garbage bin around?"

Rahul said, "Yeah, I can see a couple of them near the toilets, i.e. towards our left. Go ahead."

Aryan went towards the garbage bins but returned quickly. Seeing the empty packet of chips in his hand, Rahul asked, "What happened? Did you see some ghost there?"

Aryan said, "No, no! The garbage bin is overflowing, with muck flowing all around. I cannot dare to go anywhere near that."

Rahul mumbled, "What is happening to the 'Clean India' mission? It was re-launched by the Prime Minister amidst so much fanfare. Many politicians, sportspersons and film stars had enjoyed the photo-op. Every famous person could be seen smiling with a broom in hand. But situation is somewhat else at this railway station. We should not forget that this is the railway station of the capital city of our country. Imagine the situation in any small town."

Ankita was hearing his monologue. She replied, "What is the point of debating an issue on which nothing can be done? I will keep this empty packet in our jute bag for the time being."

General public could not be blamed for the ugly scene near the garbage bins because people had at least taken the initiative to dispose the trash in trash cans. The sanitation worker may not have reported on time or may have been fooling around which must have created that mess. At around 2:00 am in the night, hope appeared coming from the far end of the waiting area. There was a sanitation worker with a long broom in his hand. He was wearing a low-cut and skin-tight jeans and a body-hugging T-shirt. Familiar picture of Angry Bird was printed on the T shirt. Earphones were firmly plugged in his ears and he was swaying to some catchy tune. Even on that cold night, he appeared quite comfortable in his flimsy T-shirt. He strolled throughout the corridor; trying to clean up empty disposable cups, wrappers, napkins, etc. While doing so, his behavior could not be categorized as ideal as he was mouthing all sorts of expletives which were directed at everyone. His gait and behavior spoke of a very high level of arrogance as if he was not doing his duty but was trying to oblige the weary travelers who were trying to avoid any confrontation with him.

By the time, he finished his task the place was even filthier than earlier because of all the liquid spilt during his cleanliness drive. But he did a great favor by removing the overflowing garbage bags and replacing them with new bags in garbage bins. Aryan put the empty packet of chips in the freshly laid garbage bag.

It was 3:00 am when an announcement was made. It was not a pre-recorded voice rather the voice of some railway staff who was speaking with heavy Haryanvi accent. The audio quality of the speaker further compounded the problem for Rahul. But he could understand that his train would arrive at 5:00 am in the morning. Aryan was sleeping in the comforts of his mother's lap. Rahul looked at Ankita and said, "You appear to have taken some nap. Now, it is my turn. Give me a bed-sheet so that I can take some rest. Keep an eye on the luggage and be careful."

Ankita said, "You still have the luxury of two hours to complete your sleep. Go ahead."

Rahul took out a bedsheet and spread it on the floor. He kept the bag under his head and tried to take a nap. After getting up at around half past four, Rahul picked up the bed-sheet and kept it in the bag after folding it neatly. He then left the bag near Ankita. Aryan was still sleeping; oblivious to all the problems associated with erratic schedule of trains. He then asked Ankita, "Any latest development on the train's schedule?"

Ankita took a long yawn and replied, "No, there was no announcement. Hope the train would arrive by five."

Rahul said, "Let me go to the enquiry counter. I may get some updates."

Rahul then went to the enquiry counter to know the latest update on the train. The huge electronic board near that counter was displaying timings and platform numbers for various trains. All the trains were running late by many hours. But there was no information about Rahul's train. Rahul went near the enquiry counter   so that he could ask the railway staff. The person at the counter was trying to avoid dozing off. When Rahul asked about his train, the person said nothing and just gesticulated towards a white board. The white board; near the window; showed names and numbers of different trains, written with black marker.

Rahul could find his train from the list. It was showing that the train had been sent to the washing pit and would leave New Delhi at 8:00 am in the morning. So, they still had more than three hours to kill. Since the waiting room toilet was too dirty, Rahul decided to wait to board the train in which he would be finishing his early morning chores.

Rahul was sitting near his family. Their faces were already tired because of overnight wait and lack of proper sleep. Ankita said, "Can you do me a favor? Can you bring tea for us?"

Rahul smiled and said, "That is a good idea. We seldom buy tea inside the train. Let me go outside the station premises. There are some good looking shops near the bus stop. I hope I will get some decent quality tea."

Ankita said, "I think I have seen a Barista over there. But I am not sure if they provide 24 hour service near railway stations."

Rahul was soon walking towards the exit. There was a sprint in his feet. It may have been due to the way Ankita asked him for coffee. Alternately, it may have been because of the hope of finding a Barista shop. Otherwise, at most of the railway stations you will find yucky liquid in the name of tea or coffee.

Rahul had had to walk a long distance as the main entrance to the station premises must be at least 400 meter from the main building of the station. It was twilight so some darkness had already vanished. Many people could be seen sleeping on the sidewalks. They were trying to beat the cold weather by clinging to their tattered blankets. A group of people were sleeping just behind the car park; near what appeared to be a small bonfire. The stench from the bonfire was telling that they were burning discarded tyres to get some warmth. As Rahul was taking the shortest possible route so he had to cross many hurdles; in the form of barricades, stray dogs, sleeping beggars, some drug addicts, etc.

When he came out of the main gate, he could easily spot a Barista shop. To his relief, the shop was open. Rahul ordered two cups of coffee and a cup of hot chocolate. After about fifteen minutes, his order was served. The salesman came with three disposable glasses which were properly closed with lids and were slung on a cardboard hanger. Some sachets of sugar were also stuck in the hanger. The hanger made it easy for Rahul to carry those glasses.

Once inside the waiting area, Rahul woke up Aryan and handed him the glass of hot chocolate. Aryan jumped with joy, "Hot chocolate! That too from Barista! Thank you."

The strong aroma of freshly brewed coffee was hitting the olfactory receptors of Rahul and Ankita. It was enough to make them fully awake. Ankita took out wet tissue wipes. She gave one to Rahul and wiped her face and Aryan's face with other tissues. A full glass of coffee and a thorough wipe of the face did the magic. All of them were looking as fresh as if they had just arrived at the railway station.

8

The Train Arrives

At about quarter past six, the night was giving way to the dawn. Some natural light was reducing the effect of artificial light in the waiting area. Although the sky was not visible from inside but a little bit of pale orange glow coming through the huge window panes was indicating the sunrise. Some faint tweet of birds could be heard over the din of so many people at the railway station. Some people could be seen folding their bed-sheets and arranging their luggage. A batch of daily passengers could be seen rushing through the foot-over-bridge to board their trains.

At about seven, there was an announcement on the public address system. The pre-recorded voice announced about the re-scheduled departure of the train for which Bujhaavan and his friends had been waiting. The announcement was made alternately in English and Hindi. All of them were paying full attention to the announcement in Hindi. They could decipher that their train would be leaving at eight from platform number 16.

Suddenly, all of them sprang up on their feet. They quickly loaded their bags and suitcases on their heads and shoulders and almost ran towards the platform. While they were running, Bujhaavan said, "Hurry up, otherwise someone else may occupy our births. "

Jitan said, "But we have reserved tickets."

Bujhaavan said, "I know that we have confirmed tickets. But sometimes, some wicked people try to occupy even reserved births. It becomes difficult to make your rightful claim. I just want to avoid haggling with such people."

When they reached the platform, the train had already been placed on the platform. The staircase leading to the platform was wet because of the rainwater. Even the platform was soiled with muck because of continuous trampling by so many wet feet. The tin roof over the platform was not allowing too much light on the platform. Some of the iron beams under the tin roof showed nests of pigeons precariously balanced over them. The bases of some pillars had developed thick coats of white residue of pigeon droppings. Rows of electronic display boards; suspended from the tin roof; could be seen on either side of the platform. The boards were displaying the train number and coach number in alternate fashion. But such displays were of no use for an illiterate person; like Bujhaavan and his friends. Looking at a coolie; Bujhaavan asked, "Bhaiya, can you tell me the location of coach number S 7?"

The coolie raised his hand to indicate towards their coach. All of them followed in that direction. Before reaching near their coach, they passed from near the general compartment. There was a riot-like situation near the general compartment. Looking at that, Bujhaavan said, "We should thank our stars at getting confirmed tickets. Otherwise, we would be facing the same plight."

When they reached their allotted coach (S 7), the scene was almost similar as in the case of general compartment. But there was no sight of baton-wielding policemen. People were trying to outdo each other while entering the compartment. The gate which could hardly accommodate more than two people at a time was packed with more than five people. Some of them were carrying huge suitcases over their heads and were precariously balanced at the edge of the door. An old lady was almost squeezed between two persons while she was trying to enter the compartment. Loud wail of a child could be heard while his mother was trying to shove him through the narrow gap between the legs of a person.

Seeing that, Bujhaavan said to Narayan, "Leave your luggage and try to enter the compartment. Once you are in, try to open the emergency window. We will transfer our bags and suitcases through that window."

Narayan quickly followed the cue and made his way inside the compartment. He just grabbed the handrail and climbed atop it like a monkey. He contorted his body to squeeze himself through above the head of people; in order to enter the compartment. Once he was in, he opened the emergency window to make way for the luggage. His friends shoved the bags and suitcases through the emergency window; from outside. After that, Bujhaavan was the first to go in through the emergency window. His friends just shoved him like a huge luggage. His head was the first to go in; followed by his torso and legs in that order. Ramchander and Jitan quickly followed the suit. After that, it was mayhem near the emergency window. Many other people could be seen trying to enter through the emergency window. Looking at four legs jutting out of the emergency window; a policeman came to handle the situation. He picked up his baton and gave a hard blow on those legs. It was followed by a loud shriek of pain and agony and all those legs slithered inside the compartment. Rest of the crowd; which was trying to enter through the emergency window dissipated after seeing the swift action of the police.

Bujhaavan and his friends arranged their luggage on the side upper births. Both the upper births were full of their luggage. They occupied the lower births in haste; with two people sharing each of the two side births. They spread their legs to cover the whole birth to prevent any other from sitting there.

There was total chaos in the compartment. Most of the people were carrying too many bags, suitcases, cartons, etc. with them. Ladies were shouting at top of their voice, while their children were crying as they may not be feeling comfortable being pushed and shoved. Some people were also engaged in small bouts of fisticuffs while trying to arrange their luggage. The whole aisle was full of people who were trying to move through with heavy bags, suitcases, gunny sacks, cartons and baskets. Bujhaavan and Jitan were sitting on the birth number 7, while Ramchander and Narayan were sitting on the birth number 15. A family of nine had occupied the births from 9 to 14. There were four males and two females; along with three children in that family. The eldest male was in his sixties and his wife was about five years younger than him. The remaining male adults were in their thirties and the two women were their wives. One of the children was about five years old boy. Additionally, there were 12 years old boy and ten years old girl. The boy was wearing a cheap denim pant and a fluorescent orange colored jacket. The girl was wearing a skin tight pyjama and parrot green jacket. The elderly person was wearing kurta-pyajama and a blanket was wrapped around his torso. The male adults were wearing polyester trousers and red jackets of nylon. The ladies were wearing saris of bright colors. They had also applied copious amount lipstick over their lips; except the old lady. Thus, the family was composed of three generations. They shoved their suitcases and bags underneath the lower births and occupied the space between two births with rest of the luggage. There was a big carton, a huge gunny sack, a television and two huge bags in that space. The births in front of Narayan were occupied by six guys who were looking like college students. They were not carrying too much of luggage. Each of them was carrying a backpack; in the name of luggage. Some of them were wearing denim pants, while some others were wearing cotton trousers. Some of them were wearing leather jackets while some others were wearing nylon jackets. Most of them were sporting stubbles on their faces. All of them had earphones firmly plugged inside their ears as if they were some sort of prosthetic implantations.

The compartment appeared to be filthy; indicating that it was not cleaned properly at the washing pit. The blue covers of some seats were torn and were exposing jute and sponge from the inner layer. Two bulbs were missing from their holders but the remaining bulbs were giving sufficient light. The mirror near the window was broken. But glass panes of all the windows were intact.

Barring those students, most of the passengers in the compartment were talking in various dialects of Bihar; that too in rustic tones. However, the students were talking in Hindi with a typical Bihari accent. Hearing the conversation of people; nobody could tell that the train was still at Delhi. The compartment had already turned into an 'All Bihar Club'.

Finally, the train began its journey after what appeared to be an endless period of waiting for all its passengers. Some sense of calm was getting restored inside the compartment. Bujhaavan took out iron chains and secured the bags and suitcases with the chains and locks. Many other passengers could be seen doing the same with chains and locks. They also lifted the glass shutter over the window to have a better view of the outside world and to allow some fresh air inside the compartment. The compartment was filled up to its brim with people; with many people sitting in the aisle. Some people were also trying to get some space to sit on the reserved births but they met with stiff resistance from people who were carrying proper tickets for the reserved births.

An old man came near Bujhaavan and requested for some space to sit. Initially, Bujhaavan and his friends resisted his advances but later on Bujhaavan budged somewhat to allow the old man to sit near him. The old man showered him with all sorts of blessings as a mark of gratefulness. Narayan sarcastically asked from the old man, "Baba, why so much urgency to take a long journey at this age? People of your age should not venture out from home especially during the festival rush. You should have gone to some pilgrimage or on your final journey."

The old man replied, "Does an old man have no right to celebrate a festival with his family? One day, you will also become an old man like me. "

Bujhaavan said to Narayan, "You should behave in a proper way with an elderly person."

Then he said to the old man, "Baba, I feel sorry for his comments. Please forgive him, he still immature."

Once the train crossed the Yamuna river, the ticket checker came inside the compartment. He was a man of stocky frame in his thirties. His hairstyle was similar to the trend of the nineties; long tresses at the back. He was wearing the navy blue uniform of the railway. After checking the tickets of some other passengers, he came and sat near Jitan and asked them to show their tickets. Bujhaavan took out the printout and handed that over to the ticket checker. On being asked, Bujhaavan loudly said his and his friends' names. When the ticket checker asked for an ID proof, Bujhaavan showed his voter ID card.

Looking at his voter ID card, the ticket checker said, "Are you sure it is your voter ID? The picture is not clear."

Bujhaavan said; while trying to show a fake smile, "Sir, have a look at my name and my father's name. You must be aware that most of the voter-IDs show hazy photos. We can do nothing about it."

The ticket checker said, "It is ok but try to carry some other ID proof which may show a clear picture. I am a little bit liberal but you may find more strict ticket checkers during your journey."

Bujhaavan and his friends said in unison, "Yes Sir."

When the old man showed his ticket, the ticket checker almost yelled, "Baba, what are you doing? You are carrying a general ticket and you have dared to enter the sleeper class. This is illegal."

The old man folded his both hands in front of the ticket checker and said, "Beta, I know it is a general ticket. But a weak and old man like me does not have energy and strength to enter a general compartment. You are like a big sahib to me. I beg you to allow me to remain in this compartment. God would shower all his blessings on you."

The ticket checker did not say anything in reply and focused his attention to the family of nine which was in front of Bujhaavan. The ticket checker asked the names of passengers from that family. Looking at the 12 year old boy in the family, the ticket checker asked, "Where is the ticket for this boy?"

The male adult from the family replied, "Sir, he is just a child. Where is the need for a ticket for him?"

The ticket checker said, "You need at least half ticket for kids below 12 years of age. You are carrying just six tickets; for all the adults in your family. But you are not carrying tickets for your children. This is not allowed. You will have to pay fine for violating the rules."

The person looked somewhat worried and said, "Sir, our children are not going to disturb any other passenger in the train. We are illiterate people. We are not aware about the rules. Please try to understand our problem."

The ticket checker said, "Don't try to be too intelligent in front of me. I have seen many people like you who load many grown up children without buying proper tickets. I have to do my job. I am going to issue a ticket for your kids; along with the fine. I have to obey the rules."

Both the ladies in the family began pleading with the ticket checker, "Sir, you are the final authority. Please have some mercy on us. We are poor people and are not in a position to pay the fine."

The ticket checker then said, "Ok, you people appear to be enough experienced. You must be aware of the way to come out of such situations. Think about me. I too have a family to look after. I also need to celebrate Holi."

Hearing that, one of the men discreetly took out three notes of hundred rupees and shoved it in the pocket of the ticket checker. The ticket checker had been maintaining a poker face during that. After that, he nonchalantly walked off from the scene.

The ticket checker then asked the people without reserved tickets to sit somewhere near the toilets. When some of them refused to cooperate, the ticket checker said, "Don't try to take advantage of my flexible approach. I am trying to respect your feelings. I am trying to respect the occasion and hence allowing you guys to remain in this compartment. I could have easily thrown you off to the general compartment."

Hearing that, every passenger; without a reserved ticket; moved towards ends of the compartment.

Once he was out of sight, the ladies began talking among themselves, "Thanks god that the issue was settled without paying too much of money. Have we ever bought tickets for our children? Nobody does it. Had it not been the festival season, I would not have given a single penny to the ticket checker. But he too needs money to celebrate with his family."

Once the train left the periphery of Delhi, it was crossing through Ghaziabad. Many factories could be seen on both sides along the railway line. Almost all of them were belching out black smoke from their chimneys. The air was full of obnoxious smell of different kinds of gases. The puddles near the railway track were filled with dark water which must be full of contaminants. The boundary walls running along the railway line were full of graffiti. None of the graffiti was akin to colorful graffiti which are now being promoted in the name of street art in the city of Delhi. Almost all of them were written with white paint against the reddish background of brick walls. Almost all of them were displaying advertisements of many self-proclaimed sexologists of Ghaziabad. They were making lofty promises for childless couples and for men who may be suffering from bouts of self doubt about their manhood.

While Bujhaavan and his friends were unable to read the messages in those graffiti, the students in the compartment were paying extra attention to what was written on the walls. They were not reading the literal 'writing on the wall'. However, they were gleefully enjoying reading between those lines. One of them said to his friends, "Have you ever marked this peculiar trend whenever we cross some small city by train? You will find such advertisements on almost all the walls along the railway lines. Is it really such a big problem?"

Another student said, "Had it been true then our country would not have been at the second rank in terms of population in the world. India appears to be a land of fertile people who can produce millions of children per year."

A third student said, "I look at it from another perspective. We should thank all these knowledgeable sexologists for their contribution towards the population explosion in our country. "

It was almost the midday when the pantry staffs started to take orders for lunch. The pantry staff was wearing navy blue cotton trousers. He was wearing a shirt with light red and white checks. On top of that was the trademark blue apron. He was writing the orders on a small sheet of paper. When he came near Bujhaavan and his friends then Bujhaavan asked, "Bhaiya, what do you provide in a thali?"

The pantry staff asked, "Do you want a vegetarian meal or a non-vegetarian meal?"

Bujhaavan further asked, "First of all tell me the items in both the thalis."

The pantry staff said, "The vegetarian thali contains four chapattis, rice, dal, vegetable curry, raita, salad and pickle. The non-vegetarian thali contains chicken curry in place of vegetable curry. All other items remain the same. The vegetarian thali costs one hundred rupees and the non-vegetarian thali costs one hundred and fifty rupees."

Bujhaavan said, "This appears to be too costly. Do you have some cheaper option?"

The pantry staff said, "Yes, we also provide Janta Khana (People's Meal). It contains rice and dal and will cost forty rupees."

Bujhaavan said, "That comes within our budget. Please give us four packets of Janta Khana."

Narayan said, "Bujhaavan Bhaiya, can we at least buy one plate of the non-vegetarian meal just for a change?"

Bujhaavan said, "No way. We cannot afford to waste our money during the journey. We can always enjoy non-vegetarian food once we reach our village."

The lunch packs were served to them at about half past twelve. They quickly opened their packets and began to enjoy their meal like any hungry person would do. They were careful enough to spread a sheet of newspaper on their births to prevent it from getting soiled. After finishing their lunch, they wrapped the empty packets in the newspaper and threw the paper ball out of the window.

The family which was sitting in front of them was carrying home-made food. They took out containers of all sizes which were stuffed with puris, bhaji and mango pickles. Bujhaavan and his friends were looking at the appetizing fare with greedy eyes.

The students were served non-vegetarian plates for lunch. One of the students said, "We are lucky because we don't need to worry about managing the expenses. My father sends enough money in my account. It helps me in living like a prince."

Another student said, "Hmm, make your hay while the sun shines. Once you will start to live on your own, you will understand the real value of money."

The third student made a bad face and said, "This chicken does not taste good. It appears to be stale. They must have supplied some leftover stuff from the previous day."

The fourth student said, "We should not tolerate duping by the railways. Let us go to the pantry. I need to teach a lesson to the pantry staffs."

All of them said in unison, "They are charging way too much money for this horrible food. Each customer has a right to get the real worth of his money. We have every right to complain about the bad quality of food being served. Let us go to the pantry car."

All of them marched towards the pantry car. They were also shouting some slogans. A middle-aged gentleman encountered them when they were on their way to the pantry car. That gentleman said, "What happened? Why are you guys so angry?"

When he heard the whole story, he said, "It is natural to get angry at getting bad quality food in the train. But don't try to mess with these pantry staffs. They are not going to listen to you. They are always ready to indulge in brawls at a short notice. Sometimes, it can prove to be dangerous. Try to control your anger."

But the students refused to heed to his advice and continued their protest march towards the pantry car. They must have crossed four compartments before reaching the pantry car.

The pantry car was looking like any other pantry car in the trains. Empty dinner plates and other utensils were kept on the floor of two bathrooms near the entrance to the car. Anybody would feel nauseated at the sight of dinner plates lying atop the Indian style toilet seat; with water dripping all around the floor. There was a narrow corridor along one side of the compartment. A wooden partition separated the corridor from the kitchen area. A row of racks on the right side of the corridor was stuffed with all sorts of raw vegetables, flour, rice, dal, spices, cooking oil, etc. Some cockroaches were feasting from the sacks of flour. Some huge rats were scurrying through the pantry. The bulky rats were showing the nutritious fare available for them in the pantry. Kitchen platforms could be seen on the left side of the corridor. Many gas burners were producing violent flames. Some cooks were busy in frying pakodas and cutlets for the evening snacks. Delivery boys were sitting on their haunches in the congested space below the cooking slabs. Seeing a gang of protesters, they sprang up on their legs.

One of the students said, "Where is your manager? We want to meet your manager."

One of the delivery boys said, "There is no manager. Each of us is a manager. You can talk to me. Go ahead with your complain."

The student said, "You have given stale chickens to us. Is this what we expect against our money? We want our money back."

Another delivery boy said, "Bhaiya, you are not dining in a five-star restaurant. This is what you will get while you are in a train."

Another student angrily said, "Give me the complain form. I want to complain about the food."

A delivery boy said with a certain degree of arrogance, "We don't carry complain forms with us. You are free to complain to whomever you wish. Even the minister cannot do anything in this regard."

While the debate was still going on, a burly looking cook came with a huge ladle in his hand and said, "Hey, these guys appear to be very hungry. Let us give them a sound thrashing to satiate their hunger."

Hearing that, all hell broke loose. The pantry staffs started thrashing those students. They used all kinds of weapons;

like rolling pins, ladles, rods, frying pans, etc. Some of the students could also lay their hands on various tools in the kitchen. A cook tried to hit a student with the huge ladle. The student ducked to avoid being hit, and smashed his head on the cook's chest. The cook was thrown back and banged his head against the wall. Seeing that, a pantry staff held the student's legs and succeeded in pinning him down on the floor. Two more staffs began showering stray punches at the student. Similarly, another student was being held by a pantry staff from the back and was being slapped by two more staffs. Some of the students were engaged in one-to-one fight with the pantry staffs. The students were soon outnumbered and overpowered by the pantry staffs.

After about five minutes of the scuffle, some onlookers came from the nearby compartments. Some mature persons from the onlookers tried to pacify the unruly mob. They somehow succeeded in saving the students from further thrashing. One of them said to the students, "You guys have shown your immaturity. You must take a lesson from this incident. Never ever try to mess with pantry staffs or with any other person while you are travelling. The hawkers, the coolies, ticket checkers; all of them are very united. They can make a big gang at a short notice. They don't listen to even sane arguments. You must be aware of the meaning of 'might is right'."

Finally, those students were back to their compartments. All of them were muttering under their breaths. Looking at them, Narayan asked, "Bhaiya, why are you sporting blackened eyes? Did you slip in the toilet?"

Hearing that, one of the students just jumped towards Narayan to grab his collar. Bujhaavan came in between them and said, "Bhaiya, it is very easy to vent your anger on the weak. Where was all this bravura when you were inside the pantry car?"

The student meekly retreated to his seat. After that, a prolonged spell of calm prevailed in the compartment. The students were nursing their hurt egos.

9

The Journey Begins

Meanwhile, Rahul must have answered at least 20 phone calls from various relatives who were enquiring about the latest status of the train. Everybody was showing sympathy with him because of his plight. Finally, at about 7:00 am the public address system made the announcement Rahul had been waiting for. The announcement was as follows:

"Attention please, Train number 12345 Freedom Fighter going from New Delhi to Darbhanga is coming shortly on platform number 16. The train will leave New Delhi station at 8 hour zero minute. The inconvenience caused is deeply regretted."

Aryan just sprang up and his face radiated happiness because he was going to his grandfather's place. They trudged their luggage near the escalator. A person was standing near the escalator. He was trying to encourage his wife to take the escalator. But his wife appeared to be afraid to do so. She was clenching at her husband's hands. Their children were giggling while seeing the frightened face of their mother. The children were almost running through the escalator. After too much cajoling, the lady somehow agreed to use the escalator. While she was being taken to a new level of heady experience on the escalator, she was praying with her clenched eyes and fists. All the while, her husband was holding her as firmly as was possible at a public place.

Escalators have been new editions to this railway station. This has definitely helped many people because carrying heavy luggage through stairs is really difficult task. But you will find very few takers for escalators; because most of the people who come from hinterland are not comfortable at using an escalator.

They reached a foot-over-bridge after hitching a ride on the escalator. The foot-over-bridge was full of people. Almost all of them were running in a single direction; towards the platforms. After crossing about 20 m on the foot over-bridge, Rahul and his family reached the staircase which led to the platform 16. All the trains which go to Uttar Pradesh and Bihar depart from platforms 16 or 17. The electronic display board under the roof of the bridge was displaying the positions of different compartments of the train. Rahul glanced at the display board to understand the position of the coach in which he had to travel. After that, he turned towards the staircase on the left. The platform was choked with people. Majority of the people appeared to belong to the labor class as they form a major chunk of migrants to Delhi. All of them were weary eyed because of night-long sleep deprivation. All the benches were occupied by people. Whatever empty space was left on the platform; after numerous shops and vendors; was choc a block with people. Many people could be still seen sleeping on the platform. From the display board; Rahul came to know that he needed to cross five compartments to reach the bogy A3 for which he had got his ticket. When they crossed two compartments, they witnessed a huge pandemonium. It was a general class compartment and many people were shoving each other to enter the compartment. Police personnel were trying to control the crowd by application of lung power, brutal force and some waving of batons.

Seeing the crowd, Rahul took out his wallet and kept it in the front pocket of his jeans. His mobile phone was already in the front pocket. He did this as a precautionary measure to prevent pick-pocketing. Rahul and his family somehow managed to pass through that crowd to finally reach their compartment. Reservation charts had already been pasted near the entrance to the compartment. The yellow board above the windows was displaying the train number and name. Some motifs were made on the board in Mithila Painting style. In fact, the folk art of the Mithila region is known by this name. The area around Darbhanga is known as Mithila. Mithila has got a great prominence in the famous epic Ramayana. Rama's wife; Sita; belonged to Mithila. The yellow board was contrasting well with light blue background of the compartment's body. Window panes of the compartment were clean; showing that the train had just come from the washing pit. Even the yellow grab-rails near the gates were gleaming because of the adequate cleaning.

In this compartment also, people were trying to outdo each other to win the imaginary race of who finishes first. There was a long duration of about 40 minutes before the train would start but most of the people showed unnecessary urgency probably because of their sense of insecurity. Most of the people travel once or twice in a given year. Such people are usually nervous about missing their train or missing their luggage or missing their near and dear ones in the melee. The doorway was blocked because of heavy suitcases piled up near it. Some people did not even show the patience to allow elderly and children to enter the compartment. Since Rahul had travelled a lot during his stint in sales; he was as calm as ever and waited for the initial rush to fizzle out. Rahul's ticket showed birth numbers 17, 18 and 20 which meant that they had been allotted two lower births and one middle birth. He thanked his stars for not getting a side birth. During festival rush in the trains, many unauthorized passengers try to sit on the side birth; along with the passenger who is the actual passenger for that birth. Most of the people usually cooperate because they probably understand the pain of travelling with an unreserved ticket.

When Rahul reached near the allocated births, there was no space to sit. Another family who had been allotted the remaining three births in that slot was yet to arrange its luggage properly. They were carrying a little too many bags and baggage. Rahul helped them in arranging their luggage and managed to keep his luggage as well. Huge suitcases were shoved under the lower births. Handbags were suspended with hooks near the window. Jute bags were kept under the collapsible stool near the window; between the two opposite births. The collapsible stool provided ideal place to keep water bottles. Rahul took off his shoes and shoved them under the birth. He took out a pair of sandals from the jute bag and put on them. Ankita took out her slippers and put her shoes in the jute bag. Aryan preferred to keep on wearing his shoes. After that, Rahul secured the suitcase with chain and lock; by entangling the chain with the hook underneath the lower birth.

Finally, they could get some sense of calm because their much awaited journey was about to begin. When every passenger in the compartment settled to normalcy a sense of calm prevailed in the compartment. Rahul thought of using the toilet before it becomes too filthy due to overuse. Rahul was the first to go. After coming back he said, "The bathroom is quite clean right now. This is the right time to use the bathroom before it becomes too filthy."

Ankita was the next to use the toilet. But Aryan was not willing to go. He said, "I don't like to use the toilets in a train. It can be too filthy."

Ankita was trying to convince him, "The train will take too long to reach our destination. You never know when the pressure would be too much for you."

Aryan was trying to be adamant and said, "No way, I know how to hold on. I can hold on for a couple of days."

Ankita tried to explain, "It is not good to hold on. You may get cramps in your abdomen. You may even fall sick. Do you want to fall sick during Holi?"

Aryan appeared to agree and said, "Nobody wants to fall sick during Holi. Ok, you win."

After that, Aryan followed the suit and finished early morning chores. They were looking hale and hearty. There was hardly any sign of the last night's agonizing wait on their faces. It was probably because of the sense of relief and happiness to begin their journey. When you achieve even a little against all odds then you tend to forget all the pain.

The coach appeared to be reasonably clean; showing that the train was sent to the washing-pit after it arrived at Delhi station. The seat covers were sky blue in color. Pouches for keeping sundry items were of the same color and were on the partition at the back of each birth. The reading lights were closed by firmly clasping lids of gleaming stainless steel. Such reading lights were present near each tier of births. The partition above the top births was made of wire meshing. There were two small ceiling fans; which were looking like table fans. Two such fans were present between the three-tiered births, while one such fan was in the aisle near the side birth. There was a large mirror at the wall; just above the window. The quality of mirror was really good and it gave a distortion free image. Thick blue curtains were pushed to one side of the births. The navy blue curtains were matching in color with the color of the seat cover. The walls and ceilings of the compartment were of cream color. Numerous vents for air-conditioning could be seen on the ceiling of the compartment. Some motifs were made on the walls in Mithila Painting style; to give it a feel of the region of Bihar where the train was headed for.

Finally, at 8:00 am sharp; the train began leaving the platform. There was no familiar sight of people at platform waving their hands in goodbye because of the highly altered train schedule. None of the passengers was left with a friend or relative who could have enough patience or affection to wait for 8 to 10 hours just to say goodbye to a person going on a long journey. The train was slowly leaving the city of Delhi. Within a few minutes, some buildings near Connaught Place could be seen. The Statesman Building in red sandstone showed the old style of architecture. The LIC building showed the modern architecture. The Gopal Bhavan was showing even more contemporary style. Against the backdrop of buildings from the colonial era and from the post independence period, a huge tricolor could be seen fluttering in the sky; showing its pride for being the tallest structure in the area. The huge tricolor was a new addition. It was installed by some NGO being organized by a topnotch industrialist of the country.

Within five minutes, one could see the buildings of Pragati Maidan on the right side and the building of the Police Headquarters on the left side. The smiling face of Mahatma Gandhi adorned the huge façade of the Police Headquarters. Pyramidal buildings in the Pragati Maidan were reminding of many picture postcards from the capital of India. The eight-lane road passing through under the bridge did not have much traffic because Delhites begin their day somewhat late; unlike the people of Kolkata or Mumbai. After that, the train crossed over the Outer Ring Road which was followed by a bridge over the river Yamuna. The characteristic dark water was flowing through the river. The dark color has nothing to do with any folklore or mythology related to Yamuna rather it is due to very high level of pollution in the river. On the left side, one could see another bridge playing hide and seek through the mist. A metro rail was going towards eastern side of Delhi through that bridge. Many small farms could be seen along the flood bed of the Yamuna. Rows of cabbage and cauliflower were visible in those farms. After crossing the river, the train was passing through the midst of a slum. Small houses dotted the landscape. They were made of all sorts of materials; like corrugated tin sheets, asbestos, plastic sheet, tarpaulin, wood from discarded packing boxes, etc. But one could see dish antennae jutting out from most of the houses. Those dish antennae were telling the story of relative affluence even in those slums. A very wide drain was flowing through the slum. It was full of filthy water which was almost black in color. Some people were squatting on the banks of the drain; busy in early morning ablution. Some stray dogs were waiting for their turn to gorge on the fresh shit.

Ankita was busy on her phone; sharing the good news that the train had finally began its journey. Most of the listeners were hardly interested as they were also fed up of waiting to hear the progress on train's schedule. However, some close relatives felt pity at them and were worried about the remaining part of the journey. Rest of the births in that section was occupied by another family in which husband and wife were from the same age group as Rahul and Ankita. Their elder son was about 7 years old and their daughter was about three months old. The gentleman was a lanky fellow with long nose and thick moustache. His moustache was similar to those sported by south Indian film stars. He was wearing a khaki colored cotton trouser and a denim jacket. His wife appeared to be a typical desi woman with lots of love handles which enhanced her earthy charm. Her hairs were neatly tied in long braids; with pink colored hair clamp at the tip of her braid. The kohl lining in her eyes made them to appear bigger than they actually were. The small nose stud had a glittering stone which was radiating small flickers of light. She was wearing an onion colored sari with matching blouse and accessories. While her daughter was enjoying a good sleep; she was busy on her phone. Rahul was wondering at the patience of the person taking her call because she was going on and on about trivial matters. Her husband was busy on his smart-phone; playing candy crush. His son was busy on another phone; playing some racing game.

Rahul was thinking, "It is understandable for a small kid to enjoy a video game. How come grownups enjoy playing childish games like candy crush? I never play video games probably because I had had enough of it when I was in my twenties. Probably it was because I joined a job at an early age and could afford to indulge myself in such games. Even Aryan appears to have had enough of video games. He is now more interested in watching videos on piano lessons."

In one of his books; Rajneesh had mentioned that only the kings and rich people become ascetics because they could be in a position to see the futility of too much indulgence. They probably develop a sense of detachment over a period of time. Rajneesh has given many examples to prove his point. Siddhartha was a prince who gave up everything and became the Buddha. Gandhi must have come from a rich family to afford to go abroad for higher studies. Some people may not have enjoyed certain indulgences; like video games or street food; when they were kids or teenagers. They fulfill their unfulfilled dreams when they grow up. This could be the reason that most of the students in engineering and MBA colleges spend too much time on watching movies on their laptops. It is altogether a different matter that they cajole their parents to buy a new laptop for ease of study. This can be the reason that while many youngsters in India are wasting time in playing video games or in watching movies, some teenagers in the western countries are busy creating great websites like Facebook or great companies like Microsoft. We are still busy harping about number of Indian employees in those companies.

When the train was crossing the eastern part of Delhi, the ticket checker came inside the compartment. He was wearing a black coat which contrasted well with the white shirt underneath. A brass badge was prominently displaying his name. He appeared to be in his late fifties. His puffy eyes and double chin could help anyone to guess his age. The salt and pepper moustache and side whiskers accentuated his mature look. His weather beaten face also told the tales of many tortuous train journeys he must have taken throughout his long career. He was wearing a dark brown woolen cap on his head and had tied a navy blue muffler around his neck. Somehow, the woolen cap and the muffler did not go well with his blazer. He was chewing some cheaper brand of pan masala which was evident from the bad stench emanating from his mouth.

He was holding many sheets of paper which contained the reservation chart. He sat on the side birth and asked everyone to show the ticket. Rahul took out his mobile phone and showed him the soft copy of ticket. His co-passenger was also carrying the soft copy of the ticket in his smartphone. The lady on the side birth was carrying a printout of the ticket. She said, "You never know when your mobile battery is going to get discharged. My husband gave me this printout to be on a safer side."

The ticket checker did not even bother to ask for the ID proofs of the passengers. But looking at Aryan's size, he paused for a moment and asked from Rahul, "Sir, if I am not wrong you have bought a half ticket for your son. How old is he?"

Rahul smiled and said, "He is just eight years old; well within the bracket to be still eligible for a half-ticket."

The ticket checker said with an expression of surprise on his face, "Are you sure about his age? Actually, some people give false information in order to save some money."

Rahul took out Aryan's identity card and showed that to the ticket checker and said, "He is my son, so I must always be sure about his age. In fact, he is showing a good growth and appears somewhat bigger than children of his age. This identity card from his school will clear your doubts."

Looking at the identity card, the ticket checker said, "I am sorry. But I have to do my duty."

Rahul took back the identity card and said, "It's ok."

While the ticket checker was busy in checking tickets, about three or four people were almost running behind him. They tried to say something in his ears to which he never gave a reply. After he was through with the checking, he said to those persons, "Try to understand. This is the rush for Holi. There is no vacancy in this train. I am unable to manage even a single birth for you guys."

One of those guys said, "Sir, it is urgent for us to reach Bihar. Please do something."

After that, he whispered to the ticket checker, "Psst! don't worry about the rate. We will take good care of your need. We are regulars on this route."

Hearing that, the ticket checker smiled and said, "You can go to coach number B5. Take your seats on 7 and 8. I hope that will be enough to accommodate four of you. All of them are side births."

Those guys smiled in reply and rushed towards the coach number B5.

Now, the ticket checker was at the end of that compartment; somewhere near birth number 72. The guy on that birth appeared to be from a rural background. He was in his forties and was wearing pyjama kurta which were made of coarse cotton. But his blanket was quite colorful with bold floral print. There was a huge carton safely tucked to one end of his birth. The ticket checker asked him, "What are you carrying in this carton?"

He replied, "Nothing sir, just a mixer grinder. I got it at a cheaper rate from Lajpat Nagar market in Delhi. I bought it for my wife."

The ticket checker said, "Did you book this carton as extra luggage?"

The person said, "This is the only luggage I am carrying. There is no extra luggage."

The ticket checker said, "But you are not allowed to carry cartons without a proper booking. I will have to make a ticket for this; that too with heavy penalty. Otherwise, your carton will be confiscated. Did you get my point or should I call the police?"

Even on a cold day, that poor fellow was sweating profusely. He could not say anything and just kept mumbling. Then the ticket checker said something in his ears. After that, that person took out a hundred rupees note and handed that over to the ticket checker. The ticket checker calmly shoved that note inside his pocket and left the scene. Nobody in the compartment raised an eyebrow; although most of them must have watched that daylight robbery in the name of making a ticket for 'extra luggage'.

After crossing Ghaziabad, the train attained its full speed. Faint outlines of high-rise buildings could be seen on the horizon; indicating that the train was passing through the outskirts of Greater Noida.

Most of the people were making their beds to compensate for sleep deprivation. Rahul pulled out the middle birth to hold it in horizontal position with the help of iron clamps which were suspended by thick iron chains. He also helped his co-passenger in arranging the bed. He neatly covered the birth with the white bedsheet; followed by the blanket on top. After that, he put the pillows near the window, i.e. away from the aisle. Rahul said to the lady (with the baby), "You can take the lower birth if you want. This will make you comfortable. I will go to the middle birth."

Hearing that, the lady and her husband replied, "So nice of you. It will be definitely helpful.

Thus, Ankita was sleeping on the birth opposite to that lady. The births of Rahul and his co-passenger were opposite to each other. Similarly, Aryan's birth was opposite to his co-passenger's birth. They were on the topmost births. Rahul pulled the curtains and switched off the lights to minimize the light in that make-shift cubicle of thick curtains.

Most of the passengers had pulled down the curtains so the aisle was looking like a dark blue tunnel with a series of light on the roof of the tunnel. Although it was around 10 O'clock in the morning but the whole compartment was reverberating with different sounds of snoring; as if it was a night journey. The rattling sound from the rail tracks worked like perfect accompaniment to cacophony of different kinds of snoring. Even the vendors appeared to take care of not creating noise. They knew that it was going to be a long journey and they would get more opportunities to make sales.

The train had been continuing its good run since at least four hours. The lunchtime was about to begin. By now, most of the people had had a good nap. Middle births were dismantled to make way for comfortable seating. Blankets and bed-sheets were shoved to a corner of the birth. The curtains had been pushed to the sides to make way for a clear view. Many people were chattering on endless topics. Majority of them were talking in different dialects of Bihar; like Bhojpuri, Maithili and Vajjika. Their conversations were frequently interspersed with Hindi. They were also using many English words while they were talking. Bhojpuri, Maithili and Vajjika are the main dialects of north Bihar. Rahul's co-passengers (husband and wife with two children) appeared to belong to the northwestern part of Bihar as they were talking in Bhojpuri.

Hearing their talk one could get a feeling of already reaching Bihar. This must be happening in long distance trains to any place. A person going to Chennai must get the sense of reaching Tamil Nadu the moment he enters his train at New Delhi railway station. Almost every passenger was carrying homemade food. People could be seen spreading old newspaper and paper plates to arrange the platter. While puri bhaji could be seen on most of the plates, some people were carrying the quintessential litti-chokha. Litti-chokha belongs to the Bhojpur region but is savored by most of the Biharis. While they were enjoying their brunch, a hawker could be seen making his way through the aisle.

Ankita took out a disposable plate and kept four littis in it. She poured copious amount of tomato ketchup in the plate. Ankita and Rahul began relishing the litti. Aryan wanted a packet of potato chips. Aryan's co-passenger bought a packet each of chips and cakes. As they were modern kids so they did not want to eat the boring traditional food. It was a pure coincidence that the husband wife duo was also carrying litti for lunch. After finishing the lunch, Rahul got a craving for tea. He was aware of the horrible quality of tea being sold in train compartments but in spite of that he bought a cup of tea. He just wanted to enjoy the warmth of a hot cup of tea.

After taking a sip, Rahul commented, "I always wonder on the batch to batch uniformity of tea being sold on the railway network. Throughout India, you will get the same bland taste and same bad quality. I have travelled through most parts of our country but have never found any variation in the taste of tea being sold in trains. You will fail to understand how they maintain such uniformity when it comes to serve such a bad tea."

His co-passenger smiled and said, "They are probably following the principles of TQM (Total Quality Management) or Six Sigma. I also avoid having tea in the train. Once I read a news article that said that these guys use a concoction of detergent and water color in place of milk. I sometimes buy the dark tea; which you can get while traveling through some routes."

Rahul said, "That is always better than the tea with so-called 'milk'. But the quality of tea granules is worse in any case."

After finishing the lunch, everybody appeared to become comfortable enough to pay some attention to fellow passengers. Aryan was playing with the small boy who was his fellow passenger. Rahul began talking to the person in front of him. Ankita was talking to his wife.

Rahul asked, "Do you live at Delhi or had you been to Delhi to meet some relative?"

The gentleman replied, "I am living at Delhi but we belong to Chhapra."

Rahul said, "Chhapra is a great place; associated with some of the freedom fighters. In which part of Delhi are you living?"

That gentleman told, "I am living in Rohini. I am working as a Sales Manager in the insurance sector. I am looking after the areas of Delhi, Haryana and Punjab. By the way, my name is Sanjay Singh. What about you?"

Rahul said, "I am Rahul Sinha. We are living near Saket. I am working as a Marketing Manager in a dot com company. My office is in Gurgaon. We are going to Darbhanga; to my in-laws' village. In fact, the village is about 15 km from Darbhanga."

Ankita asked that lady, "You are lucky to be blessed with a cute girl child. She must be about three months' old."

That lady smiled and said, "Yeah, she is just three months' old. Her Nana Nani and Dada Dadi could not visit us when she was born. My parents live at Balia. They would be coming at Balia station to see this bundle of joy. She is the first granddaughter in my family. I have bought new clothes for them also."

Ankita said, "They will have to face all the trouble of waiting on a cold night at the platform. But that is worth it."

There was an old couple in the adjacent section. The lady appeared to be seriously sick. She was unable to even walk properly. Her husband had to accompany her to the toilet. Both of them appeared to be in their late seventies. The husband was playing an ideal nurse to the lady. But most of the time, the lady was quite rude at her husband. The old man still maintained his jovial self and scoffed at her every rebuke.

The lady could be often heard telling, "You will never learn certain things. You don't know how to pour water in a tumbler."

The husband usually replied, "With a great lady holding my reins what was the need to learn all those silly things."

The guy on the upper side birth was in his twenties. He was busy with himself. He was playing some music on his smartphone; with earphones firmly plugged in his ears. He was also looking at his laptop and was typing intermittently. Some of the books he had spread around him gave a hint that he was a student of engineering.

There was a lady on the lower side birth. She was in her early forties. She was wearing a dark blue sari with matching accessories. All the while she was keeping to herself. She was also sobbing from time to time. Ankita mustered up some courage to go near that lady and asked her, "What is the matter? You appear to be very sad."

The lady; in blue sari; replied, "Actually my father is sick. He is on his deathbed. My brother has admitted him to a nearby nursing home in Darbhanga. I don't know if I will be able to reach in time; before he leaves this mortal world."

Ankita tried to empathize with her and said, "Have some faith on the almighty. Deep in my heart, I can see that you will be able to meet your father in time. But why are you going alone? What about your family members?"

That lady said, "In fact, my daughter is preparing for her board examinations which are scheduled just after Holi. My mother-in-law also lives with us in Delhi. She is too old and we cannot leave her alone. My husband has stayed in Delhi to take care of his mother and our daughter. I am worried because this is the first time I am traveling alone."

Ankita said, "Don't worry about traveling alone. Women are more powerful than men. Now-a-days, women are also traveling to space so there is nothing to worry while traveling by train. We are here to help you in case you need."

After that brief moment of introductions and 'breaking the ice' moments, everybody was mum; looking at the vast swathe of greenery outside. Clusters of human settlements were passing by whenever the train passed through villages. Sometimes, road appeared to be going almost parallel to the rail track. Some of the car drivers could be seen trying to race with the train; forgetting that it was a race of non-equals. The power output of a car can never come anywhere close to the power output of a train engine. The car drivers may also have forgotten about frequent railway crossings which were zooming past the train at full speed.

The lady with the baby had come out of her world of the mobile phone because her baby was crying for her attention. She checked the diaper to find it needed to be changed. The lady asked her son, "Can you do me a favor? Can you take out the pack of diapers from the bag?"

"Yes Mom!" Saying that the little boy quickly climbed to the upper birth where some bags had been kept. He used the iron ladder on the side of the birth and climbed in a style which would even put Tarzan to shame. He opened a bag and took out a diaper and handed that over to his mother.

After that, the lady asked him for the feeding bottle. The boy obliged by taking out the feeding bottle. He also took out the carton of milk powder. His father; Sanjay; took out the thermos flask and poured some hot water in the feeding bottle. Then he prepared the baby's food. Once the nipple of the feeding bottle went in its mouth, the baby stopped crying. She was just enjoying herself by throwing her tiny hands and legs in all directions. Her father neatly made a small bed for her in the middle of the birth by arranging a thin cushion over a plastic sheet. Her mother then put the baby on that bed.

Looking at that child's activities, Ankita said, "Your son appears to have developed a good bonding with his sister. Sometimes, children throw tantrums after the birth of a sibling. They don't like the idea of their monopoly getting broken."

Mrs. Sanjay laughed and said, "Yeah, initially he showed predictable behavior. But gradually, he understood the worth of a baby in the family. He always cooperates with me and takes good care of his sister."

Then she caressed her son's hairs and said, "You are my good boy. Love you my son."

When the baby was through with her feeding time, she once again began to cry. Mrs. Sanjay told her son to take out the pacifier. The little boy once again climbed to the upper birth; using the ladder; and took out a pacifier. But the pacifier was empty. The boy took out a bottle of sanitizer and wiped the pacifier with it. The sanitizer emanated a strong fruity smell.

Looking at that, Aryan said, "Hey, mom this is similar to the sanitizer I got from my school."

Ankita said, "This type of sanitizer has become a craze among school kids. Initially someone distributed free samples of sanitizer in my son's school. After that, every child could be seen carrying sanitizer bottle to school. Now, they press their parents to buy a new bottle of sanitizer the moment the old one gets finished. How funny. Isn't it?"

Rahul said, "I must appreciate the sales guy who was able to convince the school teachers and all the kids about the utility of sanitizer. When I was a child, we used to play with bare feet and that too on bare ground. By the time children in those days were through with playing, their clothes, hands, face, etc. got soiled with all sorts of dirt and germs. But we never gave a hoot to all this sanitizing business."

Sanjay said, "But you should also remember that children in those days used to fall sick too often. It was probably because of the germs they collected while playing in the open. It could also be due to a poor level of hygiene. But look at the kids of these days. They have become so aware that they have already started carrying sanitizer."

Meanwhile, the little boy filled the pacifier with a fresh supply of honey and handed it over to his mother. His mother put the pacifier in her baby's mouth. Now, the baby appeared to be pacified properly; as she once again began playing, throwing her limbs and creating funny sounds in between.

10

At the Halfway Mark

After the train had crossed Tundla, the rains stopped. The sky was looking clear blue with a few stray clouds glowing in the afternoon sun. The white fluffy clouds were shining against the blue background. The whole landscape was looking like perfect wallpaper on a computer screen; which glows from the inside. You rarely get to see a clear blue sky in cities. All you get to see instead is different shades of grey in the sky. This happens because of a high level of air pollution. The perpetual smog does not make for a pleasant skyline. Most of the distant buildings are faintly visible. If you are lucky to visit the countryside then you may get a chance to witness the real blue in the sky; the blue which is usually visible in landscape paintings.

Suddenly, a rainbow appeared in the distant sky. Most of you must have seen rainbows but this was special. We normally see a fraction of a rainbow most of the time. This happens because the buildings and other man-made structures block our view. But here was a very big canvas in the form of open countryside. There was nothing between the viewers and the rainbow. One could see almost the complete semi-circle across the sky. It was really huge in size and was looking magnificent. Everybody was shrieking with child-like abandon. People were frantically clicking pictures of the rainbow. Some others were taking selfies; with rainbow in the background. Aryan also took a selfie with the rainbow. He also asked his parents to be a part of the frame. Some people were even making video of the beautiful spectacle which nature had to offer. Whenever a cluster of trees or a cluster of huts appeared to come under the base of the rainbow the huts and the trees appeared to be diffused with colorful light. The swaying trees appeared like dancers under spotlights on a stage. The whole atmosphere was looking surreal. The grand show of the rainbow must have continued for about 20 minutes. It was one of those once in a lifetime moments which everyone wants to preserve for posterity.

The lady; in the blue sari; was showing no interest in the rainbow. This was understandable as she was going to meet her dying father. She was just staring blankly out of the window and was sobbing intermittently. A while ago, she was having some homemade puri sabji for lunch when she received a phone call. She was just uttering some monosyllables while answering that call. Once the phone call was over, she did not finish her lunch and put her lunch packet back into her bag. Ankita had asked, "Is everything all right?"

Then the lady had replied, "His condition is deteriorating very fast. Even the doctors have refused now. They have told my brother to start praying to the god and to wait for the inevitable."

The lady said, "It was very difficult to get the ticket. I had given a thousand rupees extra to a neighborhood broker in order to get a confirmed ticket. I should have booked a flight ticket instead of getting a ticket for this horrible train. At least I should have been with my father by now."

Rahul said, "You never know, sometimes even the flights are delayed due to bad weather. This year's winter had continued for far too long. I don't remember when I last saw foggy mornings during the month of March. Moreover, a commute from Patna airport to the bus stand or railway station can be tough for a lonely lady. Furthermore, one also needs to keep in mind the travel time between Patna and Darbhanga. You cannot do anything as there is no flight connectivity from Darbhanga."

Ankita said, "Have some faith on your destiny. If the God is on your side, you will definitely be able to meet your father."

Most of the people had completed the much needed sleep by now. So, all of them were appearing relaxed. People who were having the privilege of a seat near the window were enjoying the wonderful landscape outside. One could see green and golden hues across the farms. It was time for ripening of the wheat crop; so golden palette was the predominant one. Clusters of trees on the horizon made olive green background; contrasting well with the golden hue of wheat farms in the foreground. The beautiful countryside was dotted with small clusters of houses at frequent distance. Children appeared to be amused at seeing scarecrows in the field. Most of them must have seen the photos of scarecrows in their books only. Some of them may have seen them in similar situations, i.e. while travelling by trains or buses. When Aryan saw a couple of peacocks; he rushed to take a snap. Sighting peacocks is quite common when you cross Uttar Pradesh by train. They are so beautiful that most of the people simply love to see them; no matter how many times they have seen the peacocks in their life.

There was an artist sitting on one of the lower side births. He was in his late twenties. He was thin and his face was adorned with sunken eyes, a pointed nose and thick lips. The remaining part of his face was hidden behind his overgrown beards which were unkempt. He had taken out his sketch book and was busy making sketches of the people, scarecrows, mango orchards, peacocks, tractors, bullock carts, culverts, and what not. Seeing an artist making sketches is quite rare for most of the people unless they happen to live near an arts college. You can see many artists in Varanasi making live sketches; especially on the numerous ghats on the Ganges. This is due to the arts college which comes under the BHU (Benares Hindu University). There was a small crowd trying to see the artist in action. While the crowd mostly contained children, there were some adults too. The artist appeared to be oblivious to all the attention and was busy in his own world.

A middle aged man asked, "Are you a painter?"

The artist mumbled, "Yes, I am a painter."

The middle aged man further asked, "But what do you do for a living?"

The artist replied, "I make paintings. I have just completed my BFA (Bachelor of Fine Arts) from BHU. I have just started my career as an artist. I have already done some solo exhibitions at some of the leading art galleries in Delhi."

The middle aged man could not get his answer. He further asked, "But what do you do for a living? I mean to earn money?"

The artist said, "I make paintings for a living; as simple as that."

The middle aged man said, "But my daughter also makes paintings. You know she had made ten paintings just after completing her graduation. She learnt that by attending painting classes in my neighborhood. Her paintings were so beautiful that it helped us in quickly finalizing her marriage with a suitable groom. But after her marriage, she never tried her hands at painting. Please give me your mail ID so that I can send the photos of her paintings."

The painter did not utter a single word in reply. He just kept mum. He probably understood common people's ignorance about painting as a profession. For most of the people from the middle class, getting a cushy job in the government is the idea of earning a living. Some people also consider starting a shop as a lucrative proposition. These occupations guarantee a regular source of income. Very few people consider artistic pursuits as serious occupation.

Rahul looked at his watch. It was half past four; the time his train would have reached its destination had it been running as per the schedule. But they were still more than six hundred kilometer away from their destination. There was a lull in the compartment. People were probably weary of talking, of fiddling with their mobile phones, of looking at the landscapes and even of observing their co-passengers.

By evening, the train was approaching Allahabad railway station. The train was chugging along at snail's pace when it was entering the platform; which is the norm at most of the big railway stations. High pitched calls of vendors; selling various items; could be heard above the cacophony of huge crowd which is a norm at most of the big railway stations. The platform was still wet; showing the proof of plenty of overnight rain. The wet tin roofs over foot-over-bridges were glowing in the evening sun. Finally, when the train came to halt, most of the male passengers went out on the platform. Rahul also wanted to enjoy some fresh air and the ambience of a world outside the confined space of an AC compartment. Moreover, he also wanted to buy something to eat.

When Rahul was going outside, Ankita said, "Try to get some guavas. The guavas of Allahabad are very famous. We never get such tasty guavas in Delhi."

Rahul's compartment was quite far from the engine; almost at the rear end of the train. So, he was unable to find a guava seller. He could see only a few vendors selling their wares near the compartment. A wheeling cart was selling magazines, comics and novels. Rahul bought a magazine on business affairs. Rahul was not sure about the duration of stoppage so he did not want to move too far from his compartment. He could see the usual items being sold. There was a vendor selling boiled eggs. Many people were buying boiled eggs. People often buy boiled eggs because of two reasons. Some people just love having boiled eggs. Some other kinds of people buy boiled eggs because of their fear of eating spicy or oily things. But these vendors usually boil all the eggs in the morning and keep on reheating them throughout the day. Another vendor was whipping up eggs to make omlettes. Omlettes; with slices of bread are also quite popular. It is tasty, has filling effect and is affordable too. Omlette is freshly prepared so there is no chance of adulteration. But the quality of cooking oil can be dubious. A vendor was wearing the railway uniform which is worn by such vendors. He was carrying an oversized tray over his head. The tray was full of cardboard boxes and the vendor was shouting at the top of his voice, "puri sabji". There was a shop displaying sandwiches and burgers in glass case. The sandwich at such shops is always stale with some awful paste in the name of mayonnaise. Even the so-called burgers contain onions which must have been chopped hours back. Some shops were selling cold drink, packaged snacks, biscuits, cake slices, etc.

Rahul was thinking, "It won't be good to eat these omlettes as they use poor quality cooking oil. The sandwiches are bland in taste and must have been made many hours back. Puri sabji appear to be cold. I can always get the packaged items inside the train."

While Rahul was trying to decide on a particular food item, he could see a good crowd around a food cart. People were jostling with each other to buy food packets. Rahul went closer to have a better look. The vendor was selling piping hot food from his cart. Some people were buying what appeared to be fried rice; with some dash of grated carrot and chopped beans for a colorful look. Some people were buying samosas which were being served with green chutney. But most of the people were more interested in buying what appeared to be oversized puris. They were golden brown in color and appeared to be stuffed from inside. They were piping hot and were inviting everyone to have a bite. It was selling like hotcakes. He was selling them at fifty rupees per plate and one plate contained two puris with lots of green chutney. Rahul decided to buy those puris because they looked quite appealing. Rahul gave him a hundred rupees note and bought two plates. He thought that four puris would be sufficient for his family. When he entered the compartment, he could see many fellow travelers had also bought the same puris. It appeared to be an instant hit.

After entering his compartment, Rahul said to Ankita, "Hey, look! I have bought these puris for us."

Ankita said, "Hmm! Looks quite appealing. Let us hope it tastes as good."

Rahuk took the first bite and reacted in a strange way, "Oh my god! It is awful. I cannot even swallow it."

Ankita also tried a bite of the puri and reacted by making a bad face. She said, "This appears to be made at least four or five days back. It appears that they have re-fried it many times. I am unable to understand the ingredients of the stuffing. Even the oil appears to be rancid."

Rahul said, "We can always blame it on our bad luck. Let me throw this into the dustbin."

Seeing their horrible faces, Aryan did not even give it a try. Rahul just threw the food in the dustbin which was near the toilet of the compartment. Within no time, almost all his fellow travelers gave the same treatment to those puris. They were horrible in taste. Probably it was the rancid oil used in cooking or the strange mixture of spices and stuffing that made those puris unpalatable. Everyone was cursing that vendor but nobody dared to go with a complaint to him.

The twenty-something guy; on side upper birth told with great enthusiasm, "That vendor has taken you people for a ride. Why don't you go to complain to him?"

Sanjay said, "There is no point of complaining to him. These people don't understand the value of customer complaint. I will be a waste of time."

That guy once again said, "You should be aware about your rights. You are setting a bad example for people of my age. Had I been in your place, I would have gone and would have taken my money back."

Rahul said, "You are still a greenhorn. You probably don't know the way it happens in our country. These vendors are a united lot. Never dare to mess with them. All of them will start thrashing you like a punching bag. They can even hold the train for ransom. It is safer to forget the money than to mess with these ruffians."

Sanjay said, "You will find the same attitude among the pantry staffs. Never ever try to argue with them. All of them begin to show their brute majority at a short notice. It is better to be safe than sorry."

That young guy appeared to have understood their point of view and did not argue with them. He was just looking at them the way any wide-eyed teenager looks.

Rahul reminisced about old days when the food in train used to be of tolerable quality. He said to Ankita, "About ten years ago, things were not as bad as they are today. I still remember the paper thin rumali rotis which I had during my transit through New Delhi railway station; about eleven years ago. Can you recall Black Diamond express which runs between Dhanbad and Howrah? I have travelled a lot by that train in the past. You could get tasty samosas, gulab jamuns, pakoris, etc. on that train. Even the simple butter toast tasted great. The eatables sold by the vendors in that train were so popular that by the time you got a second thought on buying an item you could have seen its stock finish. I don't know if the quality of food is still good in that train. It has been a long time when I last travelled by that train."

Ankita said, "You can always confirm it by asking your Jija from Dhanbad."

An old man jumped into conversation with Rahul. He said, "You are right. During my days, we used to get long grain Basmati rice from the pantry car. There used to be sitting arrangement; like a restaurant; in some trains as well. We also used to get high quality Darjeeling tea; that too in teapots. Now, all you get is tea bags in disposable glasses; and the tea is of worst quality."

Another fellow traveler began to share his opinion on the subject, "That is the reason most of the people now carry homemade food with them. Still the caterers refuse to learn. I am sure they must be incurring heavy losses."

The twenty-something looking guy too jumped in the discussion, "Don't worry uncle. Their days are numbered. I have read in Economic Times that McDonald, Burger King and Pizza Hut would soon begin to supply their products in the trains. Then these caterers would end with zero sales. When good quality burgers would be available no one will even think of having this horrible food as lunch or dinner. Have you seen their chapattis? You need very sharp knife to break them into pieces."

The old man gave his expert comment, "Hundred years from now, children would read a new kind of history books. They would be taught that cruel people from America came to India and chopped the thumbs of the local samosa maker. It will be claimed that the Indian samosa were so tasty that even the Queen of Britain used to import them for her breakfast. Ha! Ha! Ha! Ha!"

Rahul was smiling deep inside. He always wondered at the ability of people to jump into discussion on any topic even in the company of complete strangers. There was a time when traveling by an AC compartment meant you needed to keep your mouth shut because of snobbery on display in such compartments. In those days, it was very costly to travel by AC and very few people could afford to do that.

Rahul got the first opportunity to travel by AC when he was about twenty two years old. He had joined a new job and was returning from a training program which was conducted at Ahmadabad. The tickets were arranged by the company which Rahul had joined. It was a Rajdhani Express which Rahul boarded at Baroda to go to Delhi. Now-a-days, even middle class people can afford to travel by AC. So, the third AC has turned into the Sleeper class of old days; in terms of having the old world ambience of the train journey in which everybody talks to everybody. Now-a-days, the sleeper class resembles a general class coach because the crowd is mainly composed of people from lower income group. Most of them come from villages and create filth all around them.

The train had departed from Allahabad. Suddenly, Rahul heard some people singing a vulgar song in very hoarse voice. Some eunuchs had entered the compartment. There were five of them. Three of them were wearing colorful saris with matching blouse and trinkets. The remaining two were wearing Anarkali style salwar suits. Such suits come with heavy frills below the waist. All of them had put on garish makeup. At the first appearance, anybody could confuse them to belong to some dance troupe of a good repute. But their awkward gait and stubble on their faces easily gave away their identity. A heady smell of alcohol and cigarette was also emanating from their mouths. The eldest of them was beating a small drum. She was wearing a fluorescent pink sari, a peacock-blue blouse of velvet and some trinkets of golden color. Her thick lips were coated with a thick layer of rose colored lipstick. Some streaks of read juice from betel were further aggravating the garishness of her lips. The remaining two eunuchs; in sari; were singing the hit numbers from Hindi movies. The eunuchs who were in salwar suits were dancing to those tunes. Their dance movement was vulgar to say the least. They were asking for money from every passenger.

Rahul and Sanjay easily parted with fifty rupees notes to see their backs as soon as possible. They could not afford to do the other way because they were travelling with their family. But the twenty year old guy straightaway refused them. He did so only at his peril. The eunuchs cordoned him and began singing obscene songs. Someone was pinching his cheek while another was blowing a kiss towards him. The young guy finally parted with fifty rupees to get out of that embarrassing situation.

Another gentleman refused to pay money to them. Hearing that, the sari clad eunuchs began to thrust their pelvis in his face. They even threatened to lift their petticoats up if he did not agree to pay the money. They said that they would not settle the issue without taking at least a hundred rupees. The person was thus forced to cough up one hundred rupees to save his honor.

An old man became so angry that he told, "I am going to call the police."

The eunuchs laughed and said, "No one from the police would dare to come anywhere near us. Go and call your dad if you can. We will make him dance to our tunes."

The old man went towards the exit gate to look for some policeman. When he could find a policeman, the policeman refused to be of any help. He said that even he was afraid of the eunuchs. That drama must have continued for about fifteen minutes. After that, the group of eunuchs left for another compartment. One appreciable aspect about their behavior was that none of them ever tried to disturb any of the female passengers.

Rahul said, "They create nuisance on almost all major routes. One I was going from Hyderabad to Kolkata. I must have spent five hundred rupees while paying to many teams of eunuchs who boarded the train on the route."

Sanjay said, "Even the policemen don't dare to say anything to them."

A middle-aged man said, "In fact, they have a deep nexus with the police. They must be giving some share to the police."

Rahul said, "It is ok to see them dancing when they visit a house after the birth of a child. But looting in trains is way too much."

Sanjay smilingly said, "With family size getting reduced to one or two children, they may not be getting too many opportunities to dance in front of a household on the occasion of the birth of a child. They are not getting good business from their old profession and hence are searching for new avenues."

Within a few minutes, the huge swathe of the Sangam could be seen on both sides of the train. This is the place of confluence of the Ganges, the Yamuna and the mythical Saraswati rivers. The wide bed of the river was flanked by even wider beds of sand. Rows of pontoon bridges could be seen in the distance. These are made by arranging cylindrical vessels in a row. These are makeshift bridges which are made for some special need. For example;

pontoon bridges are made at the Sangam during the Kumbh Mela so that the pilgrims can easily enjoy the Mela. The train was passing the old bridge over the river. Everything all around the train had acquired golden and orange hue as it was time for the sun to set. Flickering lights from some human settlements could also be seen in the distance. The rippling water was shining like glossy pearls due to reflection of the setting sun. The reflected image of the sun in water was looking like a reddish-orange cylinder.

Once the train crossed the railway bridge the driver accelerated and the train was running at top speed. There was once again a lull in the compartment. Most of the people were busy on their smartphones. Most of the guys and girls in their teens or twenties had earphones firmly plugged inside their ears. They appeared to be busy in their own world, oblivious to all the happenings around them. Throughout the journey, such guys and girls never appeared to be interested in talking to someone not with even their family members. They only talked in monosyllables; that too when they felt like eating or drinking something or like going to the toilet to relieve themselves.

Suddenly there was some noise coming from one end of the compartment. Rahul craned his neck to see the reason of the noise. There was a young man being caught forcefully by three or four people. That man was in his late twenties. He was tall and well built. His unkempt hairs and four days' old stubble gave a disheveled look to him. His clothes were crumpled and badly soiled by grime and dust. It appeared that he may not have washed his clothes for a long time. The people who were holding him were hurling all kinds of abuses and throwing some stray punches at him. Everybody was looking at them.

Hearing that commotion, Rahul told Ankita, "Keep an eye on the luggage. I have seen such incidences many times. Criminals often use this as a tactic to divert the attention of the public. They use it as a perfect foil to get away with luggage and other valuable items from train."

When the noise was becoming too much, a GRP personnel came on the scene. He tried to analyze the situation. He asked the guys who were holding that person, "What happened? Why are you beating him?"

They replied in unison, "He is a thief. He was caught stealing a bag. We somehow managed to get hold of him."

The policeman said, "But is it the way to beat a person? Are you going to kill him? You should hand him over to us; the police. The law will take care of the issue."

After that, the GRP personnel took the person in his custody and took him away from that compartment.

When normalcy returned in the compartment, Rahul heard some shrieks from some ladies. A lady shouted, "Oh my God! My handbag is missing."

Another lady shrieked, "My sandals are missing."

A man shouted, "My mobile phone is missing."

There were at least ten people who had been robbed off their valuables while all the cacophony was going on. Rahul asked Ankita, "Check our luggage."

Ankita checked everything and said, "Thanks God, everything is in place."

Rahul said, "Nothing untoward happened to us. We are lucky."

After that, another round of calm set in the compartment and the train went chugging along.

11

Crossing Uttar Pradesh

By evening, the train reached Allahabad. Before the train could come to a stop, many vendors had already entered the compartment. They were selling different items and each of them was shouting at the top of his voice to attract customers. Some vendors were carrying huge buckets of aluminium; suspended from their right elbow. Such vendors were selling chickpea masala. It was a mixture of black and white chickpeas which had been shallow-fried after being soaked in water. This is one of the quintessential street foods which you can often find in trains, in buses and on many street corners. Some other vendors were selling raw chick peas which are sold after mixing with chopped onions, chillies, ginger, salt and some spices. It can be a healthy snack and can serve as a tasty salad. Similarly, the vendors were also selling puri-sabji, samosa, guavas, papaya, etc. Bujhaavan and Jitan got down from the train; asking their friends to keep an eye on the luggage. The platform was full of people but none of them appeared to be interested in boarding this train. It is understandable because the train was headed for another state and very few people from Allahabad would be interested in going to Bihar. Had it been going to Delhi then things could be different.

Bujhaavan went near a vendor who was selling omlettes with slices of bread. A rickety table was serving as the shop. Some crates of eggs were kept in two stacks. The white eggs were shining in yellow light. A kerosene stove was strategically positioned between the two stacks of crates. The shopkeeper was briskly pumping air in the kerosene tank in order to produce stronger flame. The burner was producing the typical sound and smell which comes from a kerosene stove. A small heap of chopped onions, green chillies, and ginger was lying nearby. The bottom of the frying pan had turned black because of a long period of use over the kerosene stove. However, the inner portion of the frying pan was shining bright.

Bujhaavan ordered for four plates of bread and omlette. The egg seller was showing all his dexterity while chopping onions and while whipping up the eggs for omlette. He quickly poured the omlette mixture into his frying pan. Once the omlette was almost half-done, he put two slices of bread on top. After that, he flipped the omlette to cook it from the other side. Bujhaavan was looking at him awestruck when the vendor tossed the omlette in mid air; while flipping it. He served the dish on pieces of newspaper; which was happily lapped up by Bujhaavan. Meanwhile, Jitan was haggling with a guava seller to get a good bargain. The guava-seller was selling appealing variety of guavas which were quite large in size. He also gave a mixture of salt and spices which goes well with guava. On Jitan's request, the guava seller chopped the guavas in four pieces each.

Once Bujhaavan and Jitan were back on their seats, they started enjoying their bread-omlette. As it was piping hot, so they were barely able to take a morsel. Nevertheless, they were showing all the urgency to finish the omlette. Bujhaavan said to Narayan, "What is the hurry? Nobody is going to snatch your food from you."

Narayan replied, "I believe that 'hotter is better'. It will become soggy once it becomes cold. The real taste is in enjoying the piping hot omlettes."

Ramchander took a bite and said, "It is really yummy. No matter how much I try, I am never able to make such a tasty omlette. The taste of ginger has enhanced its appeal."

Jitan said, "These guys are experts. He must be making at least a thousand omlettes in a day. But I can bet that he cannot paint a wall as nicely as I do."

Bujhaavan said, "You are right. Everyone can be an expert in his chosen field."

After finishing their omlettes, they crumpled the sheets of newspaper in the shape of a ball and threw them out of the window. Narayan said, "Thanks god, this window is not towards the platform. I don't need to worry about hitting someone's head with these paper balls."

After that, they began to feast on the guavas. Taking a bite, Ramchander said, "This is not without a reason that people tell numerous stories on the guavas from Allahabad. These are juicy and tasty."

Jitan said, "Add this spicy mixture and it would taste like heavens."

Bujhaavan said, "Hey Jitan, can you remember the incident when we used to steal the guavas from Lalaram's orchards in our village?"

Jitan said, "Yes, I can. One day, it was my turn to climb atop the guava tree and you were on the ground to collect the guavas. When Lalaram came there shouting, I just jumped from the tree; without thinking twice. I almost broke my legs. We ran for our life. But I must salute your courage because you kept your nerves and ran with all the guavas in your towel."

Narayan gave a wicked smile and said, "I have also heard this story from my father. But he was telling that Lalaram got hold of you at the end of the day. After that, he tied both of you to a bamboo pole and gave a sound thrashing to you guys."

Bujhaavan laughed and said, "It was a small price for feasting on the freebie."

After finishing the guavas, Narayan asked one of the students, "Bhaiya, have you tried the guavas? These are the famous guavas from Allahabad. Give it a try. You will never forget its taste."

One of the students said, "A bumpkin will always remain a bumpkin. How dare you talk to me like this? In my village, nobody from the lower caste has the guts to look into my eyes."

Narayan was taken aback at this behavior. He said, "I just appreciated a good thing. It is up to you to take or refuse my suggestion. But I think, I have not said anything wrong to you?"

Ramchander said, "Your father may be a big-shot in your village. But this is not your village. This is a train. By paying the same price for a ticket as you, I also have the same rights as you. You should leave your baggage of feudalism at your village."

Sensing another trouble brewing, another student said, "I beg your pardon on his behalf. We don't like eating these traditional stuffs. We are waiting for some vendor with packets of chips and biscuits."

Bujhaavan tried to calm down the situation further and said, "Bhaiya, all of us belong to the same state. It doesn't look nice to fight among ourselves. It will give a bad name to our state. We are going to spend at the most thirty hours together. After that, we will never meet in our lifetime. Please try to enjoy the journey and avoid arguing like this. Being a literate person; which you appear to be; you should ignore some silly comments from illiterate persons."

By the time the train had left the periphery of Allahabad, the sun was about to set. The compartment was comparatively calm; with a few stray voices of people talking in hushed tones. Within a few minutes, the train was crossing the Sangam; the confluence of Ganga, Yamuna and Saraswati. Almost all adults in the train could be seen taking out coins from their pockets or wallets or handbags and throwing those coins in the holy river. After throwing the coin, each person was folding his hands to pay obeisance to the almighty. Some of the people were also shouting, "Har! Har! Gange! (Hail the Holy Ganges)."

The students; who were observing that ritualistic throwing of coins, were showing a keen disinterest in that activity. One of the students said, "I just fail to understand this. We are in the twenty first century, yet most of the people are still to come out of their blind faith."

A middle-aged man tried to counter their argument and said, "In fact, the Ganges is considered a great river not without reasons. A major portion of the northern and eastern parts of India gets irrigated by the water from this river. The whole farming in this part depends on this river. People; like you and me; are able to get our daily bread because of this river. What is wrong in worshipping such a life sustaining river?"

Another student said, "This is what is stopping our country from becoming a developed nation."

The third student said, "But I think we are almost there. We have already sent a spacecraft to the Mars. The whole world is a fan of the software professionals from India. I have heard that more than 30% of software engineers in Microsoft are from India."

The fourth student said, "You are right. In fact, India is among the top economies of the world. This is going to be the biggest car market of the world in near future."

The fifth student said, "Have you seen the metro rail in Delhi? It is a world class infrastructure. Almost all the roads in Delhi are very wide. While roaming through the roads of Delhi, you cannot say that it is a poor country."

The sixth student said, "In spite of all these, we are still a developing country."

The first student said, "As the torch-bearers of the next generation, it becomes our duty to eradicate all the social evils from this country."

While they were busy in talking about the good, bad and the ugly of their country; a group of young guys entered their compartment. There were more than ten guys in that group; all of them appeared to be college students. All of them were wearing black pyjama-kurta and almost all of them were sporting beards. While they were walking through the aisle, they were singing some sort of rhyme.

"The future is bright.

At the end of the tunnel, there is light.

To get employment is our right.

We will make it a long drawn fight."

After that, they resorted to a brief round of sloganeering and said, "We Want Unity of Students."

Whatever they were doing was not being done in normal way. They were not creating the spectacle the way any political association does. On the contrary, they were doing their act as if they had been staging some street play. They were using all kinds of gestures and facial expressions to register their point. After about ten minutes of drama, they distributed pamphlets to every passenger.

Bujhaavan and his friends said in unison, "Bhaiya, these letters are meaningless marks for us. We are illiterate people."

They got the same response from the family which was sitting in front of Bujhaavan. But one of the students reacted somewhat angrily, "You are collecting money in the name of student unity. This is not fair. We are also students but we never resort to such tactics."

The leader of that gang told with some degree of authority in his voice, "We are going to present a street play in front of some central ministers at Delhi. We are collecting this donation for that event. I don't expect anything from these poor people. But being students; it becomes your duty to support our cause."

One of the students (the passenger) said, "But can we know your cause?"

The gang leader replied, "We are fighting for the 'Right to Employment'. Majority of students do not get jobs after coming out of college. We are demanding a job guarantee from the government."

Hearing that, one of the students said, "Hmm! You are right. We are with you. But being students, we cannot give you a fat amount."

The gang leader then said, "Any amount would do."

After that, each student (the passengers) contributed fifty rupees and thus they gave three hundred rupees to that gang of street players. The group of drama actors then proceeded towards the next compartment. Once they were out of sight, Narayan innocently asked the students, "Bhaiya, I think the government is already giving hundred days' job guarantee through MNREGA. Under this program, one member from each family gets a guarantee of at least 100 days' job in a given year."

One of the students replied, "In fact, the jobs under MNREGA are meant for illiterate and poor people like you. It is below the dignity of any literate person to do such tasks. You won't understand. It is beyond your comprehension."

The train reached Varanasi at about half past eight. The public address system was making repeated announcements about the arrival and departure of different trains. Anybody could hear that most of the trains had been running way behind their schedules. Some examples of the announcements are as follows:

"Your attention please, train number 13009 from Dehradun to Howrah is running late by sixteen hours. The inconvenience is deeply regretted."

"Train number 13268 from Jodhpur to Varanasi is running late by twenty hours. The inconvenience is deeply regretted."

Hearing those announcements, one of the students said, "It appears that none of the trains is running as per its schedule. Once a train becomes late, it goes on disturbing all the other trains. The whole schedule then goes for a toss."

Another student said, "In fact, the railway has become a behemoth. It is high time the government should go for privatization of the railways."

The third student said, "Do you know that it is the largest employer in India? What will happen to all those people once railway gets privatized? Privatization is not an answer to India's woes."

The fourth student said, "I have read on Wikipedia that rail is in private hands in many European countries."

The fifth student said, "In fact, the infrastructure is being managed by the government while running of trains is done by private companies."

The sixth student said, "I think that the solution lies in introduction of bullet trains in India. It will help in reducing the travel time. India is a vast country and hence we really need bullet trains."

The fist student said, "First of all let them learn to operate the existing trains properly. They are yet to do this in efficient manner. How many people will afford the fare of bullet trains?"

Meanwhile, Bujhaavan had something else on his mind. He said to Jitan, "Let us go to the platform to buy something to eat. I don't want to eat the pantry food."

Jitan said, "Hmm! You are right. That is costly."

Hearing their talks, the students came out of their conference about reforms in the railways. One of the students said, "Listen, he is telling about the most important issue in the current context. Let us go to buy some food from the platform."

Another student said, "Yeah, otherwise we may get another round of thrashing by the pantry staffs."

Thus, all of them got down from the compartment and began looking for something to eat. Many vendors were running hurriedly on the platform; and were shouting at the top of their voice to attract customers. Some food-carts could also be seen. Bujhaavan asked Jitan, "What do you suggest for food?"

Jitan replied, "You are talking as if have too many options. In think our budget allows only one food and that is puri-sabji."

Bujhaavan said, "Hmm, you are right. Let us buy four packets of puri sabji."

Bujhaavan asked a hawker, "How much puris are there in one packet?"

The vndor said, "Each packet has eight puris, some sabji and pickles."

Bujhaavan said, "That appears to be enough for a person. Please give us four packets."

Meanwhile, the students were still trying to figure out what to eat. One student said, "We should try something trendy."

The second student said, "I don't like traditional items; like puri sabji."

The third student said, "We can try sandwich or burger."

The fourth student said, "I have never mustered up enough courage to buy burgers from outlets of famous brands. They are too costly for me."

The fifth student said, "Don't worry. You will get cheaper burgers at railway stations. But I am not sure about the quality."

Thus, they arrived at a consensus to buy burgers. The shop which was selling burgers and sandwiches was looking quite fancy. There was a glass-showcase on the front through which one could see burgers, sandwiches, samosa, pastries, etc. on different racks. Those food items were looking quite appealing in bright light of fluorescent tubes. The signboard of the shop was adorned with laminated poster of sandwiches and burgers. The food items looked even more appealing in the poster.

After buying the food, all of them were back to their seats. Bujhaavan and his friends spread a towel on the seat to prevent their seats from getting spoiled. They opened their food packets and started to have their dinner. Bujhaavan took out a puri and kept some pieces of potato on it. The vegetable contained cubes of boiled potato which were further cooked with onions and some spices, but there was no gravy. Bujhaavan wrapped the potato cubes inside the puri to make a bite-sized roll. Jitan, Ramchander and Narayan just aped what Bujhaavan was doing. Each of them was taking a bite from the roll; followed by licking the big piece of lemon pickle. Once they finished the meal, Bujhaavan took out the bottle to have water, only to find an empty bottle. He said to Narayan, "Do you know that our bottles are empty?"

Narayan said, "Oh no. I did not notice it."

Bujhaavan said, "Being the baby of the team, it was your duty to check the stock of water. Now, what to do? The train has already started leaving the platform."

Jitan said, "I should have filled those bottles from the taps on the platform. It was my fault."

Narayan said, "No problem, we can take water from the wash basin; near the toilet."

Bujhaavan said, "In situations like this I don't mind taking water from this wash basin. But all the filth near the toilet makes it an awful experience."

Ramchander said, "It appears that Bujhaavan has succeeded in imbibing the true spirit of a big city. Have you forgotten your days in the village, when we used to have water even from that filthy old well?

Hearing that, Jitan and Narayan laughed and said, "Don't worry Bujhaavan bhaiya. These empty bottles of mineral water are enough for us to make a good impression in our village."

Thus Bujhaavan and friends took their turns to drink water from the tap near the toilet. The washbasin was clogged with all sorts of filthy materials; indicating its misuse by the public. Nevertheless, Bujhaavan and his friends also filled their bottles with water from the tap.

Meanwhile, the students did not have a good experience of trying out the burger from a railway station. One of the students lifted the top half of the burger to have a look at what was inside. There was a medium-sized patty which was dark brown in color and was oozing with oil from its pores. Thin shreds of onions; on top of the patty were emanating obnoxious smell. It was indicating that the onions must have been chopped a long time back. There was a thin slice of tomato which appeared soggy. A watery red liquid was smeared all over; in the name of tomato ketchup. To add insult to injury, the bun was a plain one which is normally used for 'Vada Paav'. Since they were hungry hence they somehow finished those burgers. After finishing their meal, they stopped a hawker to buy some bottles of mineral water. While buying the mineral water, one of the students said to the vendor, "Hey, why don't you keep mineral water from reputed brands?"

The vendor replied, "This is what is available in the train. Next time, get a five-liter bottle before boarding the train; if you are so particular about a brand."

The second student said, "There is no need to argue with these guys. Just buy what is available."

Most of the passengers were having dinner at around same time. They were showing hurry so that they could compensate for sleep deprivation of the previous night. Barring a few stray cases, none of the passengers had bought the dinner from the pantry. Most of them were carrying home-made food. Some of them had purchased something from the platform when the train was at Varanasi.

A gentleman; sitting on the birth number 23 was quite conspicuous because of the way he got ready to have dinner. He took out a plastic mug, a soap case and a hand towel, and went to the bathroom. After coming from the bathroom, his face radiated because of a thorough cleansing by soap and water. After that, he took out a comb and styled his hairs which were wet with water. Then he completed his grooming by sprinkling copious amount of talcum powder underneath his shirt. Then he took out his food from a plastic box. He sat cross-legged on his birth and neatly spread a towel on his lap. Then he began to enjoy his supper; with spoon and fork to make for a complete dining experience.

Looking at him, one of the students said, "Sir, you don't appear to be a Bihari. You must be a Bengali; if I have guessed it right."

The gentleman replied, "Yes, I am a Bengali by origin but I am born and brought up in Bihar. But what gave you the clue?"

The student said, "No Bihari; worth his salt; can follow so much etiquettes while having dinner; not even at his home."

The gentleman gave a hearty laugh at that comment.

After about an hour, the passengers were arranging their beds. The students lied down on their respective births. Each of them used his bag as a pillow but none of them used anything to cover the birth. Each of them was wearing nylon jackets to beat the cold. When one of the students got up to switch off the lights, Narayan said, "Please don't switch off the light. I need to keep awake to guard our luggage."

The student asked, "What is the need?"

Narayan said, "We are not travelling in AC compartment. All kinds of people enter and leave the sleeper class compartments during the journey. You never know which of them could be a criminal. I will advise you too to mind your luggage."

The family; which was in front of Bujhaavan's seat was facing all sorts of difficulty in accommodating within their quota of births. One of the top births was fully occupied with their luggage. The space between the two births was also full of bags and cartons. The old man in the family climbed to the vacant birth at top and started snoring within no time. The old lady occupied a middle birth. Two male members tried to adjust on one of the lower births. They were lying with one's head juxtaposed against another's feet. The width of the birth was not enough even for their lean frames. Similarly, their wives shared the opposite lower birth. The remaining middle birth was occupied by the three children who were traveling with them. The ladies gave one blanket to the old man and covered the children with another blanket. Both the blankets were quite colorful; with floral patterns all over them. The remaining adult males managed with their nylon jackets while the ladies tried to beat the cold with their flimsy shawls.

This is the norm in most of the Indian families. The male members usually get preferential treatment. If the male member is an elderly person then he gets even more preferential treatment. After them it is the turn of children to get all the care. The ladies usually manage with leftovers. The leftovers can be in the form of food or any other item of comfort.

Bujhaavan and his friends did not bother to disturb their bags and suitcases which were kept on the upper births. Bujhaavan said, "Two of us will sleep at a time, while the remaining two would guard the luggage. Let me and Jitan be the first to enjoy sleeping. Wake us up after about three hours. After that it will be your turn to sleep. The jackets we are wearing are enough to keep us warm."

There was a lull in the compartment as most of the passengers were either asleep or were trying to sleep. Some of the lights were still on and hence the inside of the compartment was glowing with pale light. Stray cries of babies, interesting sounds of snoring, siren of the train, etc. were interrupting the relative calm in between. The sounds of snoring appeared like the beginning of a piece of music. The constant rattling of the railway track was akin to the sound of percussion instruments. Intermittent sound of the siren of the train appeared to the piece when the music hits some high notes. Sometimes, when the train crossed a bridge the sound appeared like a music reaching its climax.

Narayan had lit a beeri to overcome the urge to sleep. He was sharing his beeri with Ramchander. Both of them were silently looking outside the window but nothing was visible because of the darkness. The cloudy sky did not even give them the luxury to enjoy the beauty of a star-studded sky.

At around midnight, the train made a brief stopover at some railway station. A person boarded the train from that station. He came looking for some space to sit or to sleep. He could find the empty space between the births on which the students were sleeping. That person spread many sheets of newspaper in that space. He made a pillow of his bag and sat down on the bed of newspaper. He was about to lie on his freshly made bed when he was rudely interrupted by Narayan, "Hey, you should know that this is a reserved compartment. You cannot enter a reserved compartment without a valid ticket. Just get up from here and look for suitable place for you."

That person replied, "Don't try to teach me. I know that it is a reserved compartment. I have to go to Chhapra and nobody buys a ticket for covering such a short distance."

Hearing that, Ramchander said, "Hmm, you appear to be a daredevil as well. Don't worry. Some policeman or the ticket checker must be around. He will teach you all about travelling in the sleeper class."

Hearing their discussions, one of the students woke up. After understanding what was going on; he said to that person, "Hey, hope your ears are working fine. Just get up from here and go to some other place. We won't allow you to sleep here."

That man appeared to be stubborn. He said, "Did I occupy your birth? Did I disturb you in any way? Just mind your business and let me sleep. I am a local and can hold your train for ransom."

Meanwhile, the remaining students had also woken up. All of them began arguing with that person in unison. Seeing that he was outnumbered by so many guys, that person meekly got up from there and began his long walk in search of some suitable place to make a new bed of newspaper for him.

After about an hour of that incident, Nayaran woke up Bujhaavan and Jitan; reminding them about their turn to guard their luggage. Then they changed roles and Narayan and Ramchander went to sleep.

12

From Uttar Pradesh to Bihar

By about half past eight, the train reached Varanasi.
Varanasi is famous for being one of the important holy
cities of India. The train stayed at Varanasi station for
about 20 minutes. One could not see too much outside the
window. Yellow light from sky high light-masts was
pervading the atmosphere. Constant rattling of the tracks
could be heard as some trains passed by. Some hawkers
entered the compartments to sell something which you
usually do not find being sold in train compartments. They
were selling toys made of wood. Those toys were made by
giving different shapes to wooden pieces. They were
decorated with beautiful colors and patterns. There were
dolls, birds, spinning tops, etc. Aryan found one of the toys
highly appealing. It was composed of a small disc on top of
a wooden rod. The disc had some thick and taut wires
suspending from it. Colorful horses were suspended from
those wires. There was a small hole in the rod through
which a thick rope was coming out. The disc rotated when
the rope was pulled. It appeared like a mini merry-go-
round. Rahul bought one for Aryan. While doing so, he
also saw a toy in the shape of mobile phone. Rahul asked

the vendor, "Hey, you are selling mobile phones as well. It looks good."

The vendor replied, "Yes sir, this is in high demand now-a-days. Many children press their parents for this toy phone. This is sturdy and cheap. It won't break on falling. Its price is just fifty rupees."

Rahul said, "Till date I have only seen toy phones made of plastic. It is the first time when I am seeing a toy mobile phone made of wood. Even you guys are keeping pace with the changing times. I will buy this for its novelty value."

After that, Rahul erupted in joy after seeing another toy. He said, "Look, it appears like a Matryoshka doll. These are the famous dolls from Russia. I was a proud owner of a similar set when I was a child. This doll opens from the middle; and contains another doll inside. This is followed by similar dolls when you further open the inner dolls."

Rahul told that vendor, "Can you show me, how many more dolls are inside this?"

The vendor obliged Rahul by opening a doll. There were four more dolls nested inside in different layers. Rahul bought a set of Matryoshka dolls as well. Looking at him, Sanjay said, "Now, I will also have to buy a doll for my son. In fact, the term 'Matryoshka' means 'little matron' in Russian language. Now-a-days, some contemporary designers in Russia even make caricatures of famous personalities in the style of such dolls."

Even after selling good number of toys, the toy-seller did not disembark from the train. He probably wanted to make a short trip to the next station. When the train began to leave Varanasi railway station, Rahul could not control his curiosity. He asked the toy-seller, "Aren't you getting down here? Do, you want to go all the way to Bihar; selling these toys?"

The toy-seller could not conceal his smile. He said, "No Sahib, I just want to reach my home. It is already 9 and I have been working since early morning. I live at Aurihar. I will get down at that station."

Rahul further asked, "Why do you come to sell toys at Varanasi station? Are there no customers at Aurihar?"

The toy-seller replied, "Aurihar is a small station. Very few trains cross from that junction. But Varanasi is a big station where many people come and go. We cannot get as many customers at Aurihar. "

Rahul then started talking to Ankita and Aryan, "Do you know when I was posted at Jaunpur, Aurihar was one of the markets where I used to go for my sales calls. This is just a small village. We used to get tasty kachauri and piping hot sabji at a roadside eatery. Whenever I happened to visit that place, I never missed those kachauris."

When the train reached Aurihar, it was already half past ten. The toy-seller disembarked from the train. The station was as calm as any small railway station remains during night. A few pushcarts of vendors could be seen on the platform. Some people were trying to sleep on empty benches on the platform. Near a wall; away from the platform; some ladies were sitting in a huddle. They were trying to beat the cold while trying to keep awake. In the darkness, they were looking as if many gunny sacks had been kept stacked side by side. The pale yellow light coming from over their head further enhanced the silhouette of that huddle. A stray dog was also trying to sleep nearby. The train left that station within five minutes.

After that, the train reached Ghazipur at around one in the night. Aryan was fast asleep as most of the other passengers. But Rahul and Ankita were lying awake. Both of them were on opposite births facing each other. He said to Ankita, "This is a small town. Once upon a time, it was famous for being the hub of opium trade during the days of British rule in India. Do you know that the famous novelist Amitav Ghosh had written a novel 'The Sea of Poppies' on this subject? I have read that novel. It is such an engrossing novel."

Ankita said, "Yeah, I also got to read it after you finished that novel. It was really interesting."

Hearing their talk, Sanjay also jumped into their conversation. He said, "In fact, I had my schooling from Ghazipur. My father was posted here. He was working as an officer in the education department. There was an opium factory near our quarters. I will tell you an interesting story about that factory. The monkeys living nearby enjoy drinking the water that flows through the nullah coming out from the factory. The water in the drain contains traces of opium which works like magic on the monkeys. The monkeys always keep lying in the vicinity. Most of them are barely able to even walk properly, not to think of jumping or running the way typical monkeys do. They are probably too sedated because of the essence of opium. Once there was a strike in the factory. The laborers did not report for work and the production was stopped. Due to that, the essence of opium stopped flowing through the drains. The monkeys were not getting their daily dose of their favorite contraband. They simply went mad. They ran berserk throughout the town; attacking anybody and everybody. Many people were injured within a couple of days. Most of the people stopped venturing out of their homes during daytime. A huge crowd of common people went to the spot where the laborers were staging their demonstrations. The laborers were threatened with dire consequences for holding the monkeys to ransom. The strike was immediately called off and normalcy returned for the town's monkeys and for the town's people."

Hearing that story, Ankita and Rahul felt an urge to laugh aloud. But they resisted their temptation as they did not want to disturb other passengers.

The train was chugging along at good pace. Its siren was sounding even louder because of the relative calm of the night. Rahul heard the voices of old couple from another side. The lady wanted to go to the toilet. She was too heavy for the old man. Rahul jumped from his birth and went to them to lend a helping hand. He saw that two ladies had already taken the responsibility of helping that old woman. The old man appeared to be too obliged at that gesture.

With his teary eyes, he said, "I have four sons and all of them are in good jobs. But none of them is willing to take care of us. We are going to our village to sell some ancestral property so that my eldest son can buy a new house. But he has no time to come with us. All of this must be the result of my previous deeds."

Rahul was unable to utter a single word. He just put his hand on the old man's shoulder and helped him to sit on the birth.

The train reached Balia at about 3 in the morning. Rahul's co-passenger Sanjay was awake. Sanjay's wife and son were also awake. They were keeping awake as they were waiting for Nana Nani of the baby. Sanjay was craning his neck out of the window to spot someone on the platform. When the train came to a halt, he went near the door of the compartment. Within a few minutes, he came along with an elderly man and an elderly woman. They were carrying a couple of bags. Sanjay was carrying a big basket (made of bamboo) which was gift-wrapped with colorful paper. They were the in-laws of that gentleman. One could see happiness oozing out of every pore of their heart. The father-in-law was wearing dark trousers, woolen coat and an olive green sweater. His head was covered with a muffler and thick glasses over his eyes completed the old world look. His dress gave a clue that he was reasonably rich even at that ripe age. He must be a pensioner who had retired after serving as high level officer in the government. The mother-in-law was wearing a light green chiffon sari. She was covering her upper body and head with a woolen shawl. All her hairs were jet black; probably because of copious use of hair dye. The old lady appeared to have a habit of taking good care of her grooming. Every pleat of her sari was perfectly in place; secured by a safety pin.

Sanjay's wife said, "Your granddaughter has given you lot of trouble."

Her father said, "When you were of her age, you gave even more trouble. But all the pain we have taken while waiting at Balia station is worth its every penny. I can now proudly claim to be a Nana of my granddaughter. I have already planned for throwing a grand feast on the coming Sunday to celebrate her passage through Balia."

 The elderly lady said, "I could not reach Delhi to see when this bundle of joy was born. She is like the goddess Laxmi for all of us. Do you know, my daughter looked similar when she was born?"

The elderly man said, "It appears that everyone in our family looks like you and your daughter, except me. I come from some alien family."

Hearing that, the lady said, "You will never mend your ways. Stop talking like that. You are no more a teenager."

Sanjay's wife was smiling on hearing their conversation. She said, "But her Dadi was telling that my baby resembles her Dadi."

The old lady replied, "When I will go to Chhapra to meet them, I will go with all the old photographs from my album. I will give concrete proof to your mother-in-law."

Sanjay was just keeping mum and was smiling.

It was a surreal atmosphere. In the dim light inside the compartment, one could see radiant faces of those four people; Sanjay, his wife, his father-in-law and his mother-in-law. The gummy smile of the baby matched with the smiles of her Nana and Nani. The little boy had an amused look on his face. His Nani was caressing his hairs. She was holding the little baby in her arms and was aping funny sounds created by the baby. The elderly couple had brought many gifts for the baby. Those items were neatly packed in nylon bags. There was a basket as well; which contained laddoos. The sheer size of the basket showed that there must have been at least five kilogram laddoos in that. After showering their blessings on the baby, the elderly couple said, "We need to hurry before the train departs."

They hurriedly left the compartment as it was time for the train to proceed further. Sanjay went up to the gate to see them off. His son was also following him. A few drops of tears rolled down the cheeks of Sanjay's wife. But those were the tears of joy.

It was about six in the morning. The orange yellow glow of the early morning sun could be seen on the horizon. Rahul could see from his window that another railway line from the far left was converging towards the line on which his train was running. The railway track was gleaming with yellowish-orange glow. There was a railway crossing; with a few vehicles waiting on either side of it. Rahul could guess that Bhatni station was going to be the next stoppage. The line from the left side comes from the Gorakhpur route. Bhatni is the junction at which the train routes from Varanasi and Gorakhpur converge. Looking at his watch, Rahul guessed that the train must have taken too long to travel between Balia and Bhatni. He muttered, "Oh my God! The train appears to be further delayed."

Bhatni is a medium sized station; neither too big nor too small. There was a sizeable crowd at the station. When the train stopped at Bhatni Junction, Rahul got off the compartment in search of something to eat. He knew that he could find some tasty pakoda at that station. After searching for a while, he could see some vendors busy in frying the pakodas. They were selling pakodas of potato, onion and cauliflower. Rahul bought three plates of pakodas which was enough for his family. The pakodas were piping hot and fresh. It had simple taste but the chutney enhanced its appeal. After getting a bad taste of puris from Allahabad, those pakodas were looking great. His co-passenger; Sanjay; also bought plenty of pakodas for his family. Rahul told his wife, "I must have crossed through this junction at least a dozen times. I have never missed these pakodas if I happened to cross this station during daytime. "

Ankita said, "But you always give lectures against street food. You always say that they are not hygienic. Then why so much love for these pakodas?"

Rahul said, "I know that even this stuff is not hygienic. You never know about the quality of cooking oil. You never know if the vendor had washed his hands before dipping them in the batter. But sometimes, you need to compromise on hygiene for enjoying the taste of some special street food. Don't worry. If you will get a bad tummy I have medicines for you. At least these pakodas are better than what the train pantry sells in the name of vegetable cutlets."

Rahul further continued, "In fact, I can make a long list of some good and cheap places to eat. Most of the food bloggers only write about the famous eateries of big cities. But I have rich knowledge about such eateries from many small towns of Bihar, Jharkhand and Uttar Pradesh."

Hearing that, Sanjay said, "You should turn into a food blogger. You can even make a television program on this topic."

Rahul appeared to be emboldened by that comment. He said, "Yeah, I have travelled to many small towns and villages. You will be surprised to get some of the great food at some of the unlikeliest places."

Sanjay said, "It has almost become a cliché to mention the same Karim and Tunde Kebabi in various coffee books and TV programs. Your work would definitely be an altogether different piece of creativity."

Reminiscing about his old days, Rahul said, "I can still remember the simple and fresh breakfast from an eatery in Gaya. It was a small outlet near a petrol pump. We used to go there in the morning before starting our day. You could get parathas and different kinds of vegetables on offer. What was surprising was the fact that they never sold the run-of-the-mill fares; like mixed vegetable, paneer butter masala, aloo gobhi, dal makhani or shahi paneer. You could easily get curries made of seasonal vegetables; like okra, eggplant, French beans, gourd, bitter gourd, etc."

Sanjay was showing a keen interest by uttering some affirmative monosyllables and by showing a positive body language.

Rahul further said, "There is a shop in Jaunpur by the name of Beniram. They sell puri sabji which contains many varieties of vegetable curries. The imarti which they sell is like the proverbial icing on the cake. You cannot get those imartis at any other place; succulent, juicy yet light on your pallet as well as on your wallet."

Sanjay said, "I think I will have to talk to one of my friends. He is a close acquaintance of a TV anchor from a famous TV channel."

Hearing that, Rahul laughed and said, "You are trying to inflate my ego."

The train took about four hours to travel between Bhatni and Chhapra. Sanjay was arranging his luggage as he had to get down at Chhapra. He was huffing and puffing while putting the luggage near the compartment's door. He was carrying too many suitcases, bags, cartons and baskets. Some addition was done at Balia station as well. His wife and son were not in a position to help him. The son was too young and the wife had to carry her baby. Nevertheless, his son was trying to help him by carrying some small bags. By the time, the train was crossing the outer signal of Chhapra station, the gentleman was through with arranging his goods near compartment's door. When the train slowed down somewhat, some coolies got inside the compartment. Many passengers got down at Chhapra station. Many births were now vacant in the compartment. Rahul was wondering that his co-passenger did not even bother to say goodbye to him. In fact, this happens most of the time. You get to become friendly with your co-passengers while on a long journey. You share your achievements and failures. Sometimes, you even share food with them. All of this helps in having a good time during a long journey. But the moment someone's destination comes, he gets busy in ensuring that nothing is left behind. While doing so, your co-passenger seldom gets the time to say you goodbye. This is how the life goes. You meet many persons during the journey of life. But very few people accompany you till the last destination of your journey.

Within a few moments, three people hurriedly came and occupied the seats which had just been vacated by Sanjay and his family. They were carrying too many bags with them. They were panting for breath. The moment their train started leaving the platform, one of them began shouting, "Oh my God! We did a great mistake."

The second person innocently asked, "What happened? Why are you shouting?"

The third person reacted as if he had just come out of a stupor, "Oh no, not again. We came here to see off our relatives and to help them in boarding the train. But we had shown so much hurry while entering this compartment that our relatives were left behind on the platform."

The first person said, "How many times I have told you to maintain your calm but you lose all your senses the moment you see a train."

The second person said, "Their luggage is with us and they must be feeling high and dry at the platform. They must be cursing us. Now, what should we do?"

The third person said, "Just call them on their mobile number. We will get down at the next station and then we will go back to Chhapra."

The first person said, "But this train is not going to stop anywhere before Hajipur."

The second person said, "Don't worry about that. I am going to pull the chain."

The third person said, "If that does not work then disconnect the hose pipe. I have taught you to do that during our college days."

Rahul smiled after listening to their conversation. He wanted to laugh aloud but resisted his temptation for fear of annoying those ruffian-looking guys.

It was about 10 am and many daily passengers had also boarded the train at Chhapra station. They were headed towards Hajipur or Muzaffarpur; to attend their offices. Some of them were also going to do the routine purchase for their businesses. The daily passengers usually buy a monthly pass to travel on a particular section. They are not allowed to enter the reserved compartments because they pay the fare of the general class.

Most of the daily passengers occupied those births which had become vacant at Chhapra station. Some of them also requested many other passengers to make some room for them to sit. Most of the long distance passengers cooperated with them.

The twenty year old guy; on the side upper birth; tried to complain, "Uncle, why do you people disturb the long distance passengers? You guys appear to be well educated yet do not obey the rules. You should not enter reserved compartments."

One of the daily passengers replied, "There is too much crowd in the general compartment. It is impossible to enter the general compartment. A passenger train also goes at around same time but it takes too much time. If I will take the passenger train then I will not be able reach Hajipur before 4 PM. I know it causes inconvenience to long distance passengers but I also need to reach my office. I am already late because this train has been late. "

Another daily passenger said, "You are still a greenhorn who is not aware about the way things happen here. Keep you rulebook with you. It will help you in passing your examinations. Even the ticket checker or railway police don't dare to argue with daily passengers."

The boy probably understood that he had dialed a wrong number. He hurriedly plugged in his earphones and began staring at the screen of his laptop.

Many daily passengers quickly made teams of four each and began to play the game of cards. They were playing a game which is known as 'Twenty Eight' in this part of the country. The game of 28 points is quite popular in this part of the country. This game is very simple and is played with top 7 cards of each type, viz. the heart, the spade, the club and the brick. In this game, the Jack has the highest value of 3; followed by 2 points for 9 and one point each for the ace and ten. The King and Queen come next in the pecking order; followed by eight and seven. The sixes are used as scoreboard, while the remaining cards are used for selecting the color of the trump card. This is such a simple game that even laymen easily learn to play. One can see farm laborers playing this game during off season in villages. The daily passengers were enjoying playing the game of cards. They were also gossiping on various topics; related to politics, sports and Bollywood. But politics hogged most of the limelight. People were divided into two groups; based on their political leanings. While one of the groups was speaking in favor of the ruling political party, another was speaking in favor of the opposition party. They were discussing grand topics of inflation, financial budget, foreign relations, US hegemony, etc.; as if they were sitting inside the Parliament of India. This showed the high level of political awareness among common people of India.

One of the daily passengers was around forty year old. He was wearing a black trouser and a half-sleeved shirt. The shirt was not tucked inside his pants; probably in an attempt to camouflage the huge tummy of that person. He was wearing a leather slipper; which gave a clue that he must be a government servant. Like many of his fellow daily passengers, he was chewing betel leaves. His mouth was full of betel juice because of which he was unable to speak properly. He just raised his mouth upwards and then asked his fellow passenger, "Have you seen Verma Ji who works in the court at Muzaffarpur?"

His fellow passenger appeared to be on the verge of retirement. He was wearing a dhoti and kurta. The dhoti was starch white and the kurta was of pale color. The dhoti kurta were made of some coarse fabric; may be khadi. That gentleman was chewing tobacco. He just spat the tobacco juice underneath the birth and said, "No, I have not seen him today. What is the matter?"

The first daily passenger was trying to pick imaginary food particles from between his teeth with the help of a toothpick. While continuing to do so, he said, "Actually, I have to go to Patna today so I will be getting down at Hajipur. There is an important document which needs to reach Muzaffarpur. I thought of handing over the document to Vermaji."

The second daily passenger then said, "Don't worry. We can check it out with the help of some betel seller or some beggar. Do you know that blind beggar who is a regular on this route?"

The first passenger said, "Yeah, I know him. He is not blind but acts to be a blind in order to succeed in his profession."

The second passenger said, "That is none of our business. But you can be sure of one thing. Almost all the office goers take a day or two off from their offices. But this blind beggar never has an off day. He is a regular at his work. I have been travelling on this route since last fifteen years and not a single day has passed when I have not met him. We usually hand over many important documents to him so that he passes it to the right person who may be sitting in another compartment. Let us wait for him."

Within about fifteen minutes, a blind beggar came; seeking alms from all and sundry. He was wearing bush-shirt with blue and white checks and a dark green lungi. His clothes had numerous dark patches of grime and grease as if they had never seen the face of a laundryman. His skin was also looking horribly soiled with dust and grime. His hairs were unkempt and so were his overgrown beards; with stray streaks of graying hairs. When he smiled, he displayed pale teeth which had been stained black with overuse of tobacco. It was not a pleasant look. But looking at him, the dhoti-clad daily passenger asked, "Hey, Buddhu. How are you? Have you seen Vermaji who works in Muzaffarpur court?"

The beggar replied, "Pranam sir. I am fine. Yes, Vermaji is in the next coach."

The first daily passenger gave him a big envelope and said, "Give this to Vermaji. Tell him that Pathakji has given this. This is urgent. Is it ok?"

The beggar slightly opened his eyes to have a careful look at the envelope and at the person who was giving that envelope. After that, he stayed still for about five minutes; flashing an expectant smile on Pathakji.

Pathakji quickly realized his mistake and gave a ten rupee note to him and said, "Take this. This is for your quota of tobacco."

Rahul was amazed at seeing that. He was cultured in the systems of an MNC where every work is done as per the rules and through proper channel. He asked the daily passengers, "How can you trust a blind beggar who is not even blind? It appears strange."

The elderly looking daily passenger replied, "This is a well developed system for people like us. These guys are more reliable than any professional courier guy. We even hand over cheques to these beggars and vendors. They know us and we know them. In fact, each daily passenger is like a family member. We develop long lasting friendships while traveling on a particular route. Many marriages are arranged in the train. Some people continue to travel daily for many months even after their retirement."

At the Doorstep of Bihar

Bujhaavan was looking out of the window when he said, "Look Jitan, morning star is shining bright."

Jitan looked in the same direction and said, "Can you remember Bujhaavan, the morning star worked like an alarm clock for us. We used to get up after seeing the morning star. It appeared to tell us the time to go for tilling the field."

Bujhaavan took a long breath and said, "I never get to see stars in Delhi. The whole sky is always full of bright light during the night."

Jitan said, "You cannot enjoy the beauty of the nature in any big city. Our village is a much better place. You can get to enjoy the greenery, the clean air, the rising sun, the bright moon."

Bujhaavan said, "Even the summer nights become comfortable because of the cool breeze in our village."

Jitan said, "There are times when I think of going back to settle in our village. But we don't get opportunities to earn much. Moreover, it is impossible to get even a semblance of respect once we are in village. During my father's generation we were tormented by people from forward castes. Now-a-days, people from backward castes have taken that responsibility; as most of the forward caste people have permanently migrated to cities. People in Delhi seldom bother you with questions about your caste. You can at least walk with your head held high."

While they were discussing sundry topics, the sky was taking a pale orange hue; with plenty of dark grey making way for bright light. The sky was gradually changing its colors and was showing a palette of different hues of red, orange, yellow and blue. Silhouettes of huts, buildings and trees were appearing more prominent due to the light which was becoming brighter with every passing second. Then the sun appeared on the eastern horizon. It was shining in all its glory. Bujhaavan and Jitan were looking at the rising sun without batting an eyelid. They appeared to be as awestruck as an innocent child. Suddenly, Bujhaavan said, "Do you know Jitan? The rising sun reminds me of which object?"

Jitan said, "How do I know unless you tell me?"

Bujhaavan said, "The rising sun reminds me of a huge cake made of cow-dung. Imagine a huge cake of cow-dung burning over a big hearth. It would appear like the rising sun."

Jitan looked at him with a sense of appreciation and said, "Well said. It appears that my friend has even started thinking like literate people. You are speaking like those wise guys who write poetry and stories. You are on your way to become a Tulsidas or Kalidas. I will tell this to your wife. She will be proud of you."

One of the students was overhearing their conversation. He said, "You are showing your harebrain even while using a metaphor. You should have used something better for metaphor. It is same as a policeman comparing the clanging of handcuffs with tweets of birds. I heard this line from some famous poet."

Bujhaavan said, "Bhaiya, you guys have gone to schools and colleges. You can use high sounding words to express something. But we are not so lucky. You should at least appreciate the fact that even a poor person can have some feelings."

The student laughed at that comment and said, "Ok, come out of your world of dreams. Try to use the toilet before it is too late."

Hearing that, Bujhaavan rushed to the toilet; only to come back within a few seconds. Looking at him, the student asked, "What happened? Is somebody inside?"

Bujhaavan said, "No, nobody is inside. In fact, the taps in both the toilets are dry. Not even a drop is coming out."

The student said, "Let me check the toilets near another end of this compartment."

The student came back after checking those toilets and said, "Oh God, this is horrible. No water in toilets. "

Looking at him, Bujhaavan said, "People like me can always manage in the open; in case of urgency. But what about you, what are you going to do?"

The student said, "Let the train reach Bhatni. We will talk to the railway staffs to refill the tanks in our compartment."

The train reached Bhatni at about half past six. When Bujhaavan, Jitan and two students got down at the platform, they began to look for some railway staff. People from many other compartments were also talking about lack of water in their compartments. A group of about forty people reached the office of the ASM (Assistant Station Master). The ASM was in all white uniform. His face showed that he was feeling sleepy. After listening to the people's complaint, the ASM said, "This is not a big station. We don't have arrangements for refilling the tanks in coaches. I cannot help in this regard."

Meanwhile, the crowd was swelling in size. People were getting restless. Many mini-conferences were taking place in the crowd as people were divided into many groups. Suddenly, one of the students climbed atop a huge pile of trunks. Those were metal trunks which are used by the railway guards while on duty. It was evident by names of guards on those trunks. The student began to shout as loud as he could, "Listen friends. This is the height of horrible customer service by the railways. The train still has to go another four hundred kilometer and there is no water in the toilet. NO WATER IN THE TOILET. There is no point in holding so many conferences among us. We need to be somewhat assertive. Let us rush to the engine of this train to talk to the driver. If he also shows the same attitude as this ASM, we will squat in front of the engine. We will not allow the train to move before resumption of water supply in all the compartments."

The rudderless ship was happy to get a captain. The public appeared to be in a mood to give full support to its self anointed leader. The whole crowd erupted in one voice, "Bravo! Let us go to the engine."

Once the crowd reached near the engine, the student said to the driver, "Driver sahib, there is no water in the toilets. This is early morning and the passengers need to use the toilets. We need your help."

The driver laughed sarcastically, "Where is the dearth of politicians in our country which propelled you to rise as a new leader?"

The student said, "Sir, I am not a leader or anything; contrary to what you think. In fact, we had gone to meet the ASM but he refused to help. So, we have come to ask for your help."

The driver said, "Do I carry water in the engine. The days of steam engine are history. This is a diesel engine which is full of diesel. Nobody would like to wipe his bottom with diesel. Don't waste my time. This train is already delayed. Do you know that it is running behind its schedule by more than 15 hours? Go to your compartments otherwise all of you will be left forever at Bhatni station."

The student had had enough of it. He once again shouted, "Listen friends, this driver is not in a mood to cooperate.

Let us go in front of the engine to prevent this train from moving further."

Everybody followed him and the crowd converged on the rail track in front of the engine. Some policemen also went there to gauge the situation. The driver was atop the front grill of the engine. He was pleading with the crowd sighting the delayed schedule of the train. But people were refusing to budge from the railway track. Meanwhile, many other railway staffs and local public had also converged near the engine to witness the drama which was going on.

This must have gone on for half an hour. Then the driver took out his walkie-talkie and called the ASM. The driver said, "Sir, this is the driver of Freedom Fighter. People have blocked the railway track. Please make some arrangement for refill of water tanks in the compartment. Otherwise, there will be a pile up of trains up to Varanasi."

Within no time, some railway staffs could be seen rushing towards the compartments; with hose-pipes in their hands. They quickly used the hose-pipes to connect the inlets with water line which was running along the track. After about fifteen minutes, an announcement was made on the public address system, "The water has been refilled for all the compartments. Passengers are requested to take their seats. This train is going to leave this station in ten minutes."

Hearing that announcement, people rushed back to their respective seats. The train resumed its journey after about ten minutes. Narayan said to that student, "Wow, you are really brave. You are a real leader. Now I can use the toilet without bothering about water in the taps."

The student tried to be modest and said, "I did not do anything special. Someone needs to take initiative in such situations. Today, it was my turn to take the initiative. Go ahead, and enjoy using the toilet. But I am sure the toilet must have become too filthy to be of any use."

Narayan said, "It is normal for people like us to use filthy toilet because we are used to live in unhygienic conditions. You appear to be from a good family. You may not even dare to peep inside the toilet. I can understand."

After a while when Narayan was back from the toilet, one of the students asked, "How is the condition in the toilet?"

Narayan said, "It is so horrible that I may not be able to explain. Even if I will be able to explain, you may not have the guts to hear it."

The student laughed and said, "No problem, go ahead."

Narayan said, "The moment I opened the door, a nauseating stench of urine and shit entered my nostrils. A huge heap of shit on the toilet seat was telling that one of the previous users was very poor at aiming the target. But it was an emergency for me so I had no other way than to sit on the 'hot seat'."

The student grimaced in horror and said, "It happens most of the time; especially when a train is on a long journey and you are traveling by sleeper class."

Narayan said, "Probably, you have not seen a general class toilet. You will jump out of the train to escape the stench."

Meanwhile, another ghastly spectacle was being created in front of Bujhaavan. The kid from that family was showing the urge to defecate. His mother spread a sheet of newspaper on a birth and asked the kid to use that sheet as a toilet seat. The kid must have eaten a lot for dinner and it was evident from the huge mass of nauseating stuff which had accumulated on the sheet of newspaper in due course of time. Most of the passengers; sitting nearby; were covering their noses with towel or handkerchief or anything they laid their hands on. The baby's mother immediately

259

wrapped the newspaper and threw its content outside the window. She then took the baby near the gate of the compartment and washed the baby's bottom. After that, everyone began to behave in normal way as if it was a routine affair for them.

So far, the train had been running at a good pace. But an hour after leaving Bhatni, the train hooted its siren repeatedly and gradually came to a halt. There was no railway station in sight. Most of the people were engrossed in their normal activities and nobody appeared to be disturbed. They were staring blankly outside the windows and were looking at vast stretches of farmland. When the train refused to budge even after about half an hour then people began to discuss the possible causes for the delay.

Bujhaavan said, "It appears that the line is not clear."

Narayan asked like a novice, "But why is the line not clear."

Bujhaavan replied as if he was an expert with the ways of the railways, "The train ahead of our train may be stationary at some point."

Narayan once again asked, "But why that train is staying at some point?"

Bujhaavan appeared to be annoyed and said, "How do I know?"

Meanwhile, many people had already got down from the compartment. Some of them were walking to and fro along the railway tracks. Some of them were just standing and looking in the direction of the engine. Some of them were sitting on the railway tracks. All of them were trying to understand the reason for the delay. They were also waiting for the guard to show the green flag; but it was of no use.

After a while, they saw the guard coming from the last coach of the train. The last coach is the guard's compartment. Someone from the crowd asked, "Hey Guard Sahib. What is the matter? Can we take some nap along the rail tracks?"

The guard was wearing white uniforms. He was carrying a register and a pen with him. A steel whistle was dangling from his neck. He was a stout and short man with a huge pot-belly. He was walking at a leisurely pace because he was not in a hurry to reach his destination. He threw a strong jet of red spit from his mouth on the railway track and said, "Some passenger threw an empty shell of a coconut near the railway crossing while a train was passing through the railway crossing about half an hour ago. The coconut shell hit a person who was waiting for the crossing to open. The impact was so severe that the person died. The local public has put a blockade on the track and is not allowing our train to move further."

Hearing that most of the people erupted in instant Oh! & Ah! After that people started holding mini-conferences among themselves. An elderly looking person said, "This young generation is reckless. What is the need of sipping coconut water during winter? He should have been careful while throwing the coconut shell."

A middle-aged man said, "People have no civic sense. They have made the whole railway track their garbage dumping site. You can easily see so many plastic bags, packets, glasses and plates strewn all around along the railway track; throughout your journey."

A young person tried to shut them up by saying, "How do you know that the coconut shell was thrown by a person of my generation? How do you know that all these plastic bags and glasses are thrown by young people only?"

Another person; who appeared like a Brahmin; said, "Let us not debate on who did it. Rather we should accept the fact that it is a sad incident indeed. It must have been written in his fate to die in that manner. I will pray to the god so that the departed soul attains moksha."

Someone else said, "Hmm, you are right. But our train is being delayed without a fault of ours. Let us hope that the issue gets resolved at the earliest. This train is already delayed by more than a day."

After about half an hour, the guard could be seen coming back. When people asked him, he smiled and said, "Go back to your seats. We were successful in pacifying the public. Our train will resume its journey within a few minutes."

People went back into their compartments. After hooting of siren from the engine, the train began to chug along. The train finally reached Chhapra at about ten. Many passengers got down at Chhapra station and many seats were vacant in the coach. But those seats were quickly occupied by many new passengers who had boarded that train from Chhapra. Most of the new passengers were daily commuters which was evident from their luggage. Most of them were male and most of them were carrying small handbags.

After leaving from Chhapra station, the train was catching up speed. A ticket checker came in the compartment and sat near Bujhaavan. After verifying their tickets, the ticket checker was inspecting their luggage. Looking at the tricycle on the top birth, the ticket checker asked, "Who is carrying this tricycle?"

Bujhaavan meekly said, "Sir, it is my tricycle."

The ticket checker made a stern face and said, "Well, do you have a ticket for it? Did you bother to book this tricycle as a luggage; while boarding the train?"

Bujhaavan said, "Sir, I did not. I am not aware that a tricycle needs to be booked as a luggage."

The ticket checker said, "I understand a passenger like you. People; like you; always feign ignorance and treat the passenger train as a goods carrier."

The ticket checker further said, "You will have to pay a fine for this; at least five hundred rupees."

Bujhaavan was pleading with folded hands, "Sir, I have bought this for my son. He is a small boy. Have mercy on me."

The ticket checker replied, "No way. Either you pay the fine or I will confiscate this tricycle."

Bujhaavan was at his wit's end. He was at the verge of breaking into tears. Then suddenly he appeared to have discovered his way out of that problem. He quickly took a hundred rupees note and clandestinely shoved the note into the palm of the ticket checker. The ticket checker instantly shoved that note in his pocket; while maintaining a poker face.

After successfully duping one prey, the ticket checker began prowling towards another unsuspecting prey. He focused his attention to the family; sitting in front of him. He straightaway reached to the carton of television and asked, "What is inside this carton?"

The young adult from the family said, "Sahib, we are carrying a television. It is cheaper in Delhi than at my village."

The elderly man from the family grinned and said, "Sir, my youngest daughter is fond of watching television serials. She has cleared her matriculation this year. We have bought this TV as a gift for her."

The ticket checker said, "Baba, you appear to be a mature person. At least you should have advised your sons to book the TV. Moreover, you are blocking the space between these births because of so much of luggage."

The ticket checker turned his eyes to the young adults and said, "This is not a trivial thing like a tricycle. This is a costly item. So, the fine will be more severe. I hope you understand what I mean."

The ladies started in unison, "Sir, we are poor people. Have some mercy on us. Please don't charge a fine from us."

The ticket checker replied, "What is the need for interrupting in between when I am talking to the male members of your family. You should respect our traditions; at least."

The ladies did not speak further and shut their mouths. The ticket checker turned towards the men and said, "Should I charge the fine or call the police? Take your pick."

Taking a cue from his father, one of the men took out a hundred rupees note and handed that over to the ticket checker. Looking at the note, the ticket checker said, "I too need to celebrate Holi with my family. You know what I mean."

It was strange to hear the moral lesson on 'tradition' from that ticket checker. While he was talking about the old tradition of women obeying the men, he had forgotten the tradition of honesty. He was more interested in following the tradition of bribe-takers which is deep rooted among many of his ilk. If some books on history are to be believed then corruption among government officials was rampant even during the days of Akbar. If you will read the longer version of Panchatantra you will instances of corruption even before the medieval period. In his famous story 'Namak Ka Daroga' Premchand had discussed on length about the prevalent corruption in the contemporary society. Most of us are used to this phenomenon and have learnt to adapt to the situation.

That man put another note of the same denomination in the hand of the ticket checker and pleaded with folded hands, "Sir, have some mercy. I am not in a position to pay more than this."

The ticket checker did not say a word. He moved on; in search of more potential targets. He appeared to be on a spree to collect as much 'donation' as possible. He must have planned to celebrate the Holi in grand style.

Once the ticket checker was out of sight, Bujhaavan and his friends were discussing the problem of corruption. Jitan said, "This is disgusting. We have no right to buy even small happiness for our family."

Bujhaavan said, "These guys are in government service and yet they ask for money. Even a beggar is better than them."

The elderly man; with the family; said, "I always keep some loose change in my pocket while traveling by train. Let them also enjoy the festival of Holi."

While they were engaged in the discussion, a policeman arrived on the scene. He poked his baton on the tricycle and asked, "Who is carrying this tricycle? Everybody knows that carrying a big luggage in the compartment is a crime."

Bujhaavan turned towards him and said, "Sahib, this is my tricycle."

The policeman said, "How dare you load this tricycle in this compartment? I will take you to the police post at the next station."

Bujhaavan did not say anything in reply. He quietly took out a hundred rupees note and slipped it in the policeman's hands. The policeman gave a cursory glance to the note and said, "It is ok. But be careful next time."

After that, the policeman repeated the same activity for the television which was being carried by the family. Before leaving the compartment, the policeman must have collected money from at least ten persons.

One of the students asked Bujhaavan, "You guys will seldom learn. Why don't you protest such attempts of daylight robbery?"

Bujhaavan said, "Bhaiya, we are poor people and illiterate too. We have not read the books on law; the way you people have. No ticket checker or policeman would dare to touch any suited-booted person. They always look for easy targets. We are like sitting ducks for them. On many occasions, I have been hackled by them when I tried to protest. I am mentally prepared to spend another five hundred rupees by the time I reach my destination."

The student then said, "Then why do you buy such items from Delhi. Whatever money you save while buying from Delhi must be spent on bribing these railway staffs. You get ignominy in the bargain. You should purchase these items in your village or in the nearby market."

Bujhaavan said, "I know that I can easily buy these items in the market near my village. But that will not give the sense of joy to my wife or children. You are still unmarried. You won't understand what it means to buy happiness for the family."

The simpleton was saying a universal truth about happiness. Such wisdom about real happiness seldom comes through books. One needs to experience the real happiness in order to understand the real meaning of happiness.

Indicating towards a peanut-seller, Jitan said, "Don't cry over spilt milk. Let us enjoy some peanuts."

Narayan called the peanut seller, "Bhaiya, can you tell the rate of peanuts?"

The peanut seller was a lanky fellow in his teens. He was wearing a torn jeans and a tattered T-shirt. A wooden crate was suspended from his neck. A small heap of peanuts was adorning the crate. Many pockets were present on the periphery of the crate. One of the pockets was filled with a mixture of salt and red pepper powder. Another pocket was filled with green chillies. A third pocket was filled with small sheets of paper; which appeared to be cut from a newspaper. The peanut seller was singing a song from an old movie. The song was about various dramatic benefits of eating the peanuts. The peanut seller said, "It is ten rupees for a hundred grams."

Narayan said, "Give us four packs of hundred grams each."

The peanut seller took out a small balance. It was composed of a small wooden stick and was suspended from a strong string at the centre. Two stainless steel plates (of the size of tea coasters) were suspended from each end of the rod. Those plates served as the pans for putting the weight and peanuts. It was a good example of handcrafted tool which appeared quite nice because of its small size. He put a weight on the left pan and some peanuts on the right pan. He made a long cone from the paper sheet and put the peanuts in that cone. The peanut seller also made small packets of the salt mixture by using small sheets of paper. He also gave one green chilly with each cone of the peanuts. Bujhaavan and his friends grabbed their cones of peanuts. The students also bought peanuts and so did the family which was in front of Bujhaavan.

Bujhaavan spread his towel in his lap and transferred the peanuts on the towel. He also opened packet of the salt mixture. He took a peanut between his thumb and two opposite fingers and snapped open the peanut shell. Pop came out the tiny peanuts with dark pink coat. Bujhaavan popped them in his mouth and started to chew on them. He touched the salt mixture with his index finger and licked his finger to get the flavor of the salt mixture. After that, he took a bite from the green chilly; and said, "There is nothing like enjoying roasted peanuts during a train journey. This is why they call them the poor man's dry fruits."

Jitan, Ramchander and Narayan were repeating the same ritual of enjoying the peanuts. Those students were also enjoying the peanuts in the same style. Some of them were also doing the elaborate ritual of removing the pink skin from the peanuts before eating them. The family; in front of Bujhaavan had spread all its peanuts on a towel and each member was enjoying those peanuts.

Narayan said, "The quality of these peanuts is not good enough. We get much better peanuts in Delhi; especially during the winter season. You will get to see many big heaps of peanuts by the roadside. They keep on roasting the peanuts throughout the day. This ensures that you get freshly roasted peanuts no matter at what time you are buying them. The peanuts are much bigger than what we get in trains."

Jitan said, "But the sheer enjoyment which one can get while eating the peanuts in a train beats everything else."

One of the students said, "I agree with you on this point. I seldom miss on indulging in this pleasure whenever I happen to travel by train."

Another student said, "During our school days, we read so much about recycling old and discarded things. I must appreciate the way the vendors in the train recycle old newspaper. I bet he has never studied a chapter on the recycling business."

Once they finished enjoying the peanuts, it was time for some cleaning up. The fragments of empty shells of the peanuts were randomly wiped off the towels and the births. Thus, the floor of the compartment was strewn with fragments of empty shells of peanuts. Looking at them anybody could make out two important conclusions. It was showing that the peanut seller was able to do brisk business. It was also showing the litterbugs in most of the passengers who were travelling in that compartment.

14

The Final Lap

The train reached Sonpur at about half past eleven. This small town is famous for the annual cattle fair which is known as Sonpur Mela and Harihar Kshetra Mela. This town is on the confluence of Gandak and the Ganges. According to folklore, Chandragupta Maurya used to come to this place to buy elephants. There is a mythological story associated with Harihar Kshetra. The story goes as follows:

"There was a king named Indrayamuna and there was a Gandharva chief named Huhu. King Indrayamuna was turned into an elephant because of a curse by the great sage Agastya. On the other hand, Huhu was turned into a crocodile under the curse by the great sage Dewala. One day; somewhere in Nepal; the elephant was caught by the crocodile. The elephant fought very hard to escape the sudden death. But when it sensed its imminent death, the elephant picked a lotus flower in its trunk and started to pray to the Lord Vishnu. Lord Vishnu appeared and killed the crocodile with his Sudarshana Chakra. Thus, the crocodile was free of its curse. Since the chakra also touched the elephant, the elephant could also be free of the curse. Lord Vishnu is also known as Hari and he took away the unhappiness from the lives of the king Indrayamuna and the Gandharva Huhu hence this place is called Harihar Kshetra. It is said that the Hairhar Nath temple in this town was built by Lord Rama while he was on his way to Janakpur. "

This is a month long fair which begins after fifteen days of Diwali. People from almost all parts of Bihar and many other parts of the country come to participate in this fair. Among the cattle sold here; elephants are the main attraction. Some people still sell and buy elephants just as a symbol of prosperity. This mela is also famous for numerous dance and magic shows which are performed by lowly paid artistes.

The platform at the Sonpur railway station is the longest platform in Bihar. In fact, before the opening of the Gandhi Setu on the Ganges; to serve as a road link between Patna and northern parts of Bihar, small ships were the only means to cross the Ganges to reach Patna. Most of the trains from different parts of north Bihar used to reach Sonpur by evening or late night. Then people used to board the small ships in hordes. The long platforms were made in order to accommodate many trains at a time.

This place is also associated with another interesting story. This is about the beginning of Sulabh International by Bindeshwar Pathak. Sulabh International is an NGO which makes and maintains toilet complexes at many public places in India. He was deeply involved with removing the malpractice of manual scavenging by people of a certain caste. There is a popular myth in Bihar related to the actual beginning of the Sulabh International. People used the banks of the Ganges for open defecation once they crossed the river from Sonpur and reached Patna. Bindeshwar Pathak was moved by seeing hordes of people sitting on their haunches all along the banks of the river. It is needless to say that those people must have been busy in relieving themselves. The ghastly sight and obnoxious smell worked as motivation for Bindeshwar Pathak to do something to provide public toilets to as many people as could be possible.

After a very brief stopover at Sonpur, the train started for its next stoppage, i.e. Hajipur. Just after leaving the railway station, the train was passing through a bridge. The bridge is over the river Gandak. The Gandak comes from the left side; while you are headed towards Hajipur. You can see the Ganges on the right side. Partly because of being a confluence of two major rivers and partly because one of the rivers is the Ganges; you can see huge stretches of water all around you. What is unique about this place is clear demarcation of water of both rivers; in terms of color. While the water from the Gandak is somewhat clear, the water in the Ganges is somewhat muddy. The water in the Ganges appears muddy because it carries more clay and debris than any other river in India. You can also see vast swathes of banana plantation along the banks; towards Hajipur side. When seen from the height of the bridge, the vast swathe of banana plantations appears as if a huge green carpet has been laid on the earth. India is the largest producer of bananas in the world and Hajipur is a major contributor towards its banana production. You can find so many banana sellers at Sonpur and Hajipur stations that you will easily understand that plenty of bananas are being produced here.

When the train reached Hajipur, Rahul was looking at his watch. It was already 12:00 noon. He told Ankita, "The way this train is going, we won't be able to make to Samastipur before four."

Ankita said, "I have seen it happening every time when the train crosses Chhapra. After Chhapra, the railway people seem to forget about the existence of this train. Then it runs at a turtle's speed."

Rahul said, "And things become worse by the time the train departs from Hajipur. Let us see, what we have in store for us."

Aryan was listening to their discussion. He chirpily said, "We should be happy and thankful to the Indian Railways. We have paid the fare for a twenty hour journey but we are getting so many extra hours to enjoy in the same train."

Rahul and Ankita laughed at hearing that comment. Many other people in the train also laughed along with them. But the laughter of almost everyone was appearing to be empty, sans any real happiness. It had more touch of satire on the way the train was getting late by every passing hour.

The lady; in the blue sari; said, "This train seems to have some enmity with me. I don't know if I will be able to reach in time. It would be a lifelong curse for me if I fail to meet my father before he breathes his last."

Ankita asked that lady, "What is the latest update on your father's condition?"

The lady replied, "His condition is not good. He is sinking very fast."

Ankita said, "Keep some hope and have some faith in the God. I have seen many examples where a firm belief in the God has worked wonders."

Many vendors entered the compartment; selling bananas. All of them were carrying a single variety of bananas; with golden skin. This is known as 'chiniya kela' in local language; meaning tiny bananas. They are very small; the size of a parval (Trichosanthes dioica). But the taste is much sweeter compared to any other variety of bananas. Any Bihari; worth his salt; would be ready to gorge on those tiny bananas at any given time. Most of the daily passengers bought those bananas. Rahul also bought them. While Rahul and Ankita enjoyed those bananas, Aryan refused to do so. One of the daily passengers commented, "These are new age children. Give them a packet of potato chips and they would trade away anything for them. Hey kid, you should eat lot of fruits as they are good for your health."

Rahul asked the twenty-something guy; on the upper birth, "Would you like to have some bananas? They are really tasty."

The guy replied, "Thank you for your offer. But I don't take food from strangers. You never know. The food can be traced with sedatives."

Rahul said, "You are talking the bitter truth. Even I have seen many people falling prey to criminals who lace edibles with sedative. The effect is so strong that the unsuspecting victim is knocked out of his senses for many hours. Many of them even need to be hospitalized. You can only have a pity on them on seeing their horrible condition."

The guy replied, "Yeah, but I have observed that most of the victims are from labor class. They are simple people and can be easily taken for a ride. Please don't mind if I have offended you by refusing your offer."

Rahul said, "No! No! It is ok. You are doing what any sane person would do."

Meanwhile a passenger came to occupy a birth opposite to the birth on which Rahul was sitting. That passenger was accompanied by a very old and frail man. The senior citizen was barely able to walk and needed all the support while trying to sit on the birth. That passenger took out a mosquito net from his bag and arranged that net over the lower birth. After making a bed for the old man, he helped the old man in lying on that bed; duly covered with the mosquito net.

Rahul was curiously watching all this. He asked that person, "I am amazed to see the perfect size of this mosquito net. Where did you get it?"

The person replied, "I gave special order to the tailor after taking careful measurement of the length and width of the birth in a train."

Rahul further asked, "He appears to be your father. He is lucky to get such a caring son. By the way, where are you headed for?"

The person said, "Yes, he is my father. We are going to Samastipur and I have bought a proper ticket for the travel."

Rahul said, "It is strange. Nobody tries to buy a proper ticket for travelling such a short distance. You appear to be a law abiding citizen."

The person said, "In fact, my father holds a certificate of being a freedom fighter. The sarpanch in my village had helped us in obtaining that certificate. Being a certified freedom fighter, my father is entitled to free travel by air-conditioned class. He is also entitled to take an attendant along with him. To take out the maximum benefit of this facility, I always take my father along with me whenever I need to travel. This helps in saving money. Thanks to my father, I have travelled to most of the parts of India. You can say that I have travelled all the way from Kashmir to Kanyakumari."

Rahul could not suppress his curiosity and asked, "How old is your father?"

The person replied, "He is seventy five years old. Why did you ask this question?"

Rahul said, "We will be celebrating 70th anniversary of freedom of India within a couple of years. This means your father was not more than five years old when India became a free country. It is amazing that he was a freedom fighter at such a young age."

The person replied, "Who cares? All you need to get a certificate for freedom fighter is to have some connection and some courage. Once a certificate is in your hand, nobody is going to ask questions. This helps a lot in saving travel bill."

Rahul was at his wit's end after hearing that answer. People find so many ways to find their ways around the maze of numerous rules and regulations.

After the train left Hajipur, banana plantations disappeared from sight. Small villages could be seen on both sides of the track. The wheat farm was showing golden yellow hue; reminiscent of the riches it was holding in the form of ripened wheat grains. A big red-colored building could be seen alongside the railway track. By its appearance, one could easily guess that it was a jail. Any local person; living outside the state usually remembers that landmark; as it marks the beginning of the heart of north Bihar. After that, there was a railway crossing through which the Patna-Muzaffarpur highway crossed. This crossing was the sign that Muzaffarpur was still about 40 km away. After another hour, the Patna Muzaffarpur highway was running almost parallel to the railway track. Then, the train passed through under a road-bridge. That road; going through above the railway line is the NH 24, the highway which goes towards Assam via Samastipur, Barauni and Purnea. The road which was going straight and somewhat parallel to the rail track goes to Muzaffarpur city. The sight of flyover made Rahul to sit upright as it was an indication that Muzaffarpur station was about to come. But soon after the train crossed through under the flyover, it came to a halt with repeated sounds of its siren. The repeated sirens showed that some miscreants must have pulled the chain so that the train could come to a halt. Rahul muttered, "It appears that someone has pulled the chain so that he can get down at his doorstep."

One of the daily passengers said, "No sir, these are the passengers from the Guard Quota."

Rahul asked, "What is this Guard Quota? I am hearing about it for the first time."

The daily passenger replied, "In fact, the guard allows some passengers to sit in his coach; in lieu of some money. Then he applies the brakes somewhere near the outer signal so that such passengers can get down from the train. Even the driver becomes an active part of this business. He just sounds the siren to create confusion that someone may have pulled the chain."

Rahul asked, "They must be making good amount of money by doing that."

The daily passenger said, "They do it for sure. There is a guard in my neighborhood. He has recently built a bungalow type house. I am sure he cannot afford to build such a palatial house from the money he gets as salary."

Rahul said, "He understands that nobody is going to complain for a delay of five minutes when the train is already delayed by about twenty hours."

When Rahul craned his neck to have a look, the signboard showed the name of Ramdayalunagar. It was a small railway station which has no stoppage for any major trains. But Rahul's train must have stayed there for at least an hour. All the passengers were cursing the rail minister. Some of them were also cursing the station master of Muzaffarpur railway station.

Rahul said, "It appears that the platform at Muzaffarpur railway station is not vacant. That is why they have stopped the train at this station."

Another passenger said, "How do you expect the platform to be vacant? Every rail minister announces many new trains in every rail budget. This route is already choc a block with trains; leaving no scope for additional train. More number of trains means more delays in running schedule of most of the trains."

A third passenger said, "No sir, this is not the fault of rail minister. Many rail ministers in the past happened to go to the Parliament from Bihar. Hence, they introduced new trains for Bihar; in order to help the people of Bihar. This is the fault of the station master. He must be negligent on his duty. I know these guys. He must be enjoying a pitcher of toddy right now; forgetting about the train."

Another passenger said, "Things were not as bad earlier. In those days, most of the trains terminated at Muzaffarpur station. After the opening of broad gauge line to Darbhanga, many trains have been extended up to Darbhanga and beyond. Situation has taken a worse turn only after that."

Rahul said, "You appear to belong to Muzaffarpur, if I am right."

The passenger replied, "Yes, you are correct."

Rahul said, "Try to think beyond Muzaffarpur. Try to think the relief which people of Mithila got after the opening of broad gauge line. This has enabled many poor people from that part to migrate to big cities; like Mumbai and Delhi."

That passenger said, "It appears that you belong to Darbhanga."

After that, both of them laughed aloud.

Finally, the train reached Muzaffarpur station at about 3 pm. All the remaining daily passengers got down at Muzaffarpur. One of them could be heard mumbling, "We need to rush to the office to make our attendance. After that, we will have to rush back to board a train back to Chhapra. All of this in the name of a day's work."

The train took three hours to cover a distance which should have been covered in an hour. But the train showed some promptness while leaving Muzaffarpur railway station. Rahul said to Ankita, "If the train does not behave notoriously then we shall be at Samastipur by four pm. We can hope to reach Darbhanga latest by seven."

Ankita said, "Let us hope, it does not."

The train was running at good speed. It crossed many small stations; such as Dholi and Silhout; without making any stopover. But it came to a halt at Karpoorigram. This small station was earlier known as Doodhpura but it was rechristened as Karpoorigram in honor of a former Chief Minister named Karpoori Thakur. Samastipur was just five or six kilometer away. At this station, the train behaved in the same way as it did before reaching Muzaffarpur. Most of the people in the train were too tired to make any comment. Everybody was mum; as if they were watching the movie 'The Silence of the Lambs'. Meanwhile, many trains coming from the other side; crossed that station at full speed. But the rail minister was probably moved by their plight and the train left that station after staying there for just half an hour.

The train reached Samastipur at half past four. Rahul was aware that the train would stop at Samastipur for about half an hour; because of a need to change the direction of the engine. Rahul asked Ankita, "Do you want to eat the famous son-papdi from Meenakshi Sweets?"

Ankita said, "I think, you are talking about the sweetmeat shop near the entrance of this station. I would love to have those son-papdis but do we have so much of time."

Rahul said, "Yeah, the train stops at this station for about twenty minutes because they change the engine. I can rush to bring the stuff within that timeframe."

Ankita said, while Rahul was moving towards the gate of the compartment, "Hurry up! Don't miss this train."

Rahul was almost running like a teenager as if he was going to buy a rose for his girlfriend. He was taking two steps at a time while climbing the stairs to the foot-over-bridge. After that, he almost ran through the bridge. Once he was near the exit gate of the station, he could see the glowing signboard of Meenakshi Sweets. There is nothing special when you look at this shop. Such shops can be found in almost each town of India. But Rahul's family members go crazy over the son-papdi from this shop. Whenever someone from the family is going to Delhi and passing through Samastipur he is requested or cajoled or ordered to come with the tasty son-papdi from that shop.

By the time Rahul was back from the sweetmeat shop, train's engine had been changed. Most of the passengers were already inside the compartment; in anticipation of a green signal from the guard. However, some passengers were still taking a stroll on the platform; in order to give the much needed exercise to their legs.

Suddenly, all hell broke loose on the platform. People were scurrying in every direction. Some people could be seen toppling over one another. It was a stampede like situation; albeit on a smaller scale.

Rahul tried to go near the gate of the compartment to have a clear picture but there were far too many people near the gate. Rahul came back to his seat and tried to assess the situation while looking through the window.

A bull was running ferociously on the platform. People were running for their lives. Most of the people could get enough time to climb the stairs to reach to the safety of the foot-over-bridge. However, some people came within the hitting range of the bull. By the time, the bull completed its horrific run through the platform at least twenty people were badly injured. Somehow, the railway police; some other staffs; with the help of some local vendors; were able to drive the bull away to an isolated place which was far from the platform.

When some sense of normalcy returned on the platform; many of the injured were helped back to their seats in the compartment. About five passengers from Rahul's compartment were also injured. On being asked they gave no clue about the cause of that accident.

That unfortunate incident delayed the train by another thirty minutes. When the train resumed its journey for its final lap, it was already half past five. Some police personnel were also sitting in the compartment. They were accompanying the injured people. It was because of those policemen that the reason of the bull's run could become clear.

The bull appeared to be a regular on the platform. This is quite common. We always witness stray cows and bulls roaming on the roads. Sometimes, a stubborn cow may end up holding the traffic for hours. Such stray animals have probably learnt to live amidst the chaos created by human beings. They seldom disturb the people because they also know the value of a peaceful coexistence. People often give leftovers for such animals to eat. Some religious minded people also offer some specially prepared food to these animals. So, seeing a ruminating cow near a person who may be busy in afternoon siesta does not raise an eyebrow of anybody in our country. You may have also seen some people stopping their car near a cow and feeding the cow through the window of the car.

The bull was probably too hungry or too curious. It approached near the foodcart of a samosa seller and poked its nose in the boiling hot oil in the wok. The hot and boiling oil must have had a devastating effect on the senses of the bull. It triggered a panic reaction in the bull and the bull began its show of corrida in order to enact the scene of

Spain right here in India. The bull was probably fed up of seeing too many picture postcards from Spain.

15

The Lady In Blue Sari

Rahul and his family must be happy by virtue of being in the final lap of their epic journey. This is evident from the way Rahul bought son-papdi from Meenakshi Sweets.

While most of the people traveling in that train were traveling for the sole purpose of celebrating the festival of Holi, many others could be traveling for many other reasons. We should not forget about the lady who was traveling to see her father who must be having a face to face conversation with Yama; the god of death.

For the sake of convenience, let us assume the name of this lady as Neelam. I could think of this name on the basis of the color of her sari.

The train was now travelling in opposite direction because of the change of engine from one end to another. Samastipur is a big junction which was evident from numerous railway tracks spanning across a huge width. The train must have changed endless number of tracks while leaving the station. Within five minutes, the train was crossing through under a foot-over-bridge; followed by a flyover. Busy market was visible on both sides of a railway crossing which appeared to be abandoned. Concrete walls could be seen blocking both sides of the railway crossing. Many people were astride their two-wheelers while they were crossing the foot-over-bridge. The approach to bridge must be having a ramp to facilitate two-wheeler's entry on it. Once the train was past the flyover, it took a steep right turn. The railway line; going towards Muzaffarpur was diverging towards the left. A dilapidated sugar mill could be seen on the right side of the track. Many old buildings could be seen in rows along the sugar mill. Those buildings appeared to be quarters for the staffs of the sugar mill. The plaster was missing from most of the buildings; showing the utter neglect. The vacant ground and paths (leading to the quarters) were full of overgrown grass and water puddles.

When the train crossed the premises of the sugar mill, it approached an iron bridge. It was crossing the river Gandak. The road bridge was visible on the distant right. Some people could be seen walking along the bathing ghats along the river bank; towards Samastipur side. It did not take long for the train to cross the bridge as it was a small bridge. After the train crossed the bridge, the rail track was passing along a high embankment. Nothing was visible on the left side because of the embankment. But mango orchards could be seen on the right side.

After about fifteen minutes of leaving Samastipur, the train stopped at a small station; named Muktapur. Neelam got a call from her brother and said, "The train has reached Muktapur. It appears that the train is not on the main line. There must be a crossing for some train."

Her brother replied, "Don't worry. Even father appears to be determined to meet you. He is somehow holding on."

The line from Samastipur to Darbhanga is a single line. So, a train needs to stop at small stations in order to allow the train from opposite direction to pass through. It was the time for many long distance trains leaving from Darbhanga. After a wait of about ten minutes, a train from Darbhanga crossed Muktapur railway station. After another ten minutes, another train crossed. After about five minutes, Neelam's train resumed its journey.

The train quickly attained speed after leaving Muktapur. The sun had already set and hence nothing was visible outside. A few flickering lights could be seen in distance whenever a small village happened to cross by. After about fifteen minutes, the train stopped at another small station;

Kishanpur. Neelam craned her neck and saw that the train was along a platform. She heaved a sigh of relief as it signaled a routine stoppage without a need for crossing of another train. The train left that station within a few minutes. The train crossed some small station within fifteen minutes and was once again accelerating. After crossing a couple of iron bridges within a few minutes, the train came to a halt at Hayaghat. It resembled like a small bazaar. Hawkers were sitting along the rail tracks and along the road which was almost parallel to the rail track. Most of the hawkers were keeping what appeared like a rudimentary table lamp. The lamp had a wooden box at the base with makeshift rod on top. Some LED lights were fixed on a rectangular board which was mounted atop the rod. The box contained small batteries which are used in two-wheelers. The whole market was glowing in colorful light coming from those makeshift table lamps. Such table lamps tell the story of the famous 'jugad'(ingenuity) in our country. They are made by local fabricators who work on a shoe-string budget and sell them at a price which is affordable to their customers.

The train must have stopped at Hayaghat for at least half an hour; allowing the crossing of three trains from Darbhanga. After leaving the Hayaghat station, the train once again crossed an iron bridge and attained its full speed. It was pitch dark outside; with no trace of light anywhere.

The train reached Laheriasarai at about seven pm. Laheriasarai and Darbhanga are twin cities with a gap of five km in between. Once at Laheriasarai, the train appeared to be refusing to go further. Neelam was getting restless. She had called her brother and told, "Are you at Darbhanga station? Is there some train to cross my train?"

Her brother replied, "Yes, I am at Darbhanga station. There is no train to leave this station. But all the platforms are occupied. Once any of these trains would leave for the washing pit, they will give green signal to your train."

Neelam said, "Should I get down and start walking along the railway track?"

Her brother said, "No need, it is already dark. It cannot be safe walking along the railway track. I know it is difficult to maintain your patience when you are so near."

Finally, at about quarter to eight the train left Laheriasarai station. It reached Darbhanga in less than five minutes after what appeared to be an endless wait. The distance between Samastipur and Darbhanga is about 40 km. But the train took almost three hours to cross that distance.

Once the train stopped at Darbhanga, Rahul helped Neelam with her luggage. He could see Neelam's brother waiting for her near the gate of the compartment. Both of them hugged each other and burst into tears. Neelam was wailing uncontrollably. Her brother was trying to calm her down. He said, "Our father is still alive. Do you remember what he said when he last talked to you on phone?"

Neelam took some breaths and said, "Yes, I can remember. He said that he would wait for me."

Her brother said, "He is really waiting! Only for you! Let us go. Only you can help him in escaping from all the pain he is going through."

Once outside the railway station, Neelam's brother started his bike. Neelam hopped on the pillion seat; firmly clasping on her bag. Her brother hurriedly negotiated through the traffic and reached the nursing home.

Once at the gate of the nursing home, Neelam jumped off the bike and almost ran inside. She went near her father. Her nephew told, "Dada, look who has come to meet you? It is your daughter, Neelam."

It was nothing short of a miracle. The old man was lying unconscious for the last four days. He was barely managing to be alive because of many life-supporting devices. He opened his eyes and looked at his daughter. Tears rolled down his pale looking eyes. Neelam was trying to hold on her tears but was unable to do so. Her father just said, "Neelu."

The monitor near his head began to show a blank and dark screen. The small room was filled with sounds of wailing and crying.

Meanwhile, Rahul was back to his seat to arrange his luggage. Ankita asked Rahul, "Is her father still holding on?"

Rahul said, "Yeah, thanks god. Her brother said so. I hope he was telling the truth. I have heard many tales of people missing interviews and even their date with marriage; because of a train running behind its schedule. But for the first time in my life I have came across such an incident."

Ankita said, "It is high time that ministers and top level officials in the railways need to think from this angle as well. But they always appear to be busy in throwing popular gimmicks in the name of reforms in the railway."

Rahul waited for the passage to become clear before taking out his luggage. His father-in-law was waiting at the platform. After coming out of the train, Rahul, Ankita and Aryan touched the feet of the old man to take his blessings. Rahul's father-in-law said, "Even Columbus would have returned without bothering about the discovery of India. You guys are really brave to complete such a tortuous journey."

Rahul laughed and said, "I was not alone. Other passengers in this train were equally brave. By the way, how are we going to proceed to Simri. Isn't it too late to get a bus for the village?"

Rahul's father-in-law replied, "Don't worry about the bus. I have already booked a taxi. It will hardly take us about thirty minutes to reach our village."

Aryan jumped with joy, "Yeah, we are going by taxi. Let us go."

16

Welcome to Mithila

Bujhaavan was looking out of the window. He could feel the lashing of the gushing wind coming through the window. The towel in his neck was fluttering violently; indicating the speed of the wind. Jitan was in front of him. Both of them were sitting with straightened legs in a way that one's legs were parallel and opposite to another's legs. While enjoying the gushing wind through the window, Bujhaavan sneezed a few times. Looking at Bujhaavan, Jitan said, "You are growing old and giving tell-tale signs by sneezing. Let us change seats so that you won't have to face the wind."

Bujhaavan laughed and said, "I am still capable of increasing the brood of my children. Let me just stay for a month in the village and I will give the result at an appropriate time."

Jitan smiled and said, "Are you planning to raise a cricket team? This is ridiculous. You should learn from the people in the city. Most of them have just one or two children."

Bujhaavan said, "I was just kidding."

Looking outside the window, Bujhaavan said, "Hey, it appears that we are approaching Sonpur. I can see the never-ending platforms of Sonpur."

Narayan called from his seat, "The moment a train reaches Sonpur, I get a feeling that I have already reached home."

Ramchander said, "You are still more than a hundred kilometer far from your home."

Jitan said, "Narayan is correct. In fact, once the train crosses Sonpur, it appears that we have entered a known territory. Everything looks so familiar. You get a feeling of reaching your own land, your own soil."

The train reached Sonpur at about half past eleven. Most of the daily commuters got down from the train. A fresh set of passengers entered the compartment and occupied the vacant seats. Bujhaavan asked his friends, "I am feeling hungry. Should we go for puri-sabji or something else?"

Narayan said, "Let us go for the bananas of Hajipur. I have not tasted the famous 'chiniya kela' (tiny bananas) since a long time."

Looking at him, Jitan laughed, "Look at this guy. He is behaving like a typical city boy. How can anybody survive by merely eating some bananas, or any other fruit? I need something which can fill my stomach."

Bujhaavan said, "Ok, I will buy some bananas for everyone. I will also buy puri-sabji; for the filling effect."

Bujhaavan got down at the platform and bought two dozens of bananas and four packets of puri-sabji. He transferred those stuffs to Jitan through the window and said, "Give me the empty bottles so that I can fill them. There is a tap nearby."

Bujhaavan filled five bottles with water and passed them to Jitan. While taking those bottles, Jitan said, "Can you buy some tobacco and beeri as well. Our stock is finished."

After about ten minutes, the train left Sonpur station. The family; in front of Bujhaavan had taken out various home-made items for lunch. Bujhaavan and his friends were busy in gorging on puri-sabji and bananas. Jitan said, "These bananas are really sweet. Given their small size, I think two dozen is too little for us."

Bujhaavan said, "We have to think about our budget as well. We cannot afford to indulge in so many items. I will get ten dozen of bananas from the orchard in our village."

Jitan said, "When did you buy an orchard? You never told me."

Bujhaavan said, "Had I been able to buy orchards, I would not have been working as a laborer at a construction site. I am talking about the orchards of Lalaram. We can always sneak in to steal some bananas."

Ramchander said, "Bhaiya, you are no longer a small boy. Leave the task of stealing from orchards to your kids."

Narayan said, "The bananas which we get in Delhi are much bigger in size. They are so filling that I can have just six of them at one go."

Ramchander said, "But the taste of 'chiniya kela' is different. It is divine."

Meanwhile, a street urchin had entered the compartment from Sonpur station. He was wearing tattered shorts which had become almost black because of the thick layer of grime. He was covering his torso with a shirt. Most of the buttons on his shirt were missing. His hairs were appearing like bunches of coarse fiber. His eyes and nose were full of dry layer of muck. That poor chap was holding a broom in his hand. Soon after entering the compartment, he began cleaning the compartment with his broom. He cleaned all the debris from under the births. He also cleaned the peanut shells, paper balls, disposable glasses & plates, empty bottles of water, etc. After clearing the debris, he carefully swept them up to the gate of the compartment. After that, he swept them off outside the compartment. After finishing the task, the boy approached each passenger for some money. Most of the people happily parted with coins of one rupee or two rupees.

While giving a five rupee coin to him, Bujhaavan said, "Good job. People like us keep on littering the compartment but people like you never complain while cleaning the filth."

A student said, "These guys have found an innovative way to beg for money. The government should put such guys behind the bars."

Another student said, "But I think the government should put these guys in schools. They must have been forced in this work because of their poverty."

After finishing their lunch, they started paying attention to some new passengers in the compartment. A young lady was sitting on the adjacent birth. She was wearing a red sari with floral prints and zari border. She was wearing silver anklets which appeared like thick rings. A similar but larger ring was adorning her neck. Her well-oiled hairs were parted at the centre and parting was daubed with plenty of vermillion. A big vermillion dot on her forehead was further enhancing her earthy beauty. There was a baby in her lap. The baby was about two years old. It was wearing bright yellow shorts and T-shirt. Thick bands of black thread were tied around the baby's wrists and ankles. Small pom-poms were dangling from those bands. The pom-poms were of red color. The baby's eyes were lined with thick lines of kohl and a black dot was made on his forehead. The mother-son duo was showing the perfect picture of lady who may be returning from her parent's place; along with her kid.

Sensing the lady to be from the same economic strata, Bujhaavan asked, "It appears that you are coming from your father's place."

The lady replied with certain degree of coyness, "Yes, I am going to my in-laws' place."

Bujhaavan smiled and said, "This is a cute baby, appears to be a boy."

The lady said, "Yeah, he is a boy."

Jitan jumped into their conversation and said, "Look at the fifty rupees note in his hand. His nana must have given this to him."

The lady just nodded her head in yes and smiled.

Bujhaavan said, "Look at the way, he is clenching at the note. I feel amazed whenever I see a small child holding on the currency note. I just fail to understand, how they know the value of money."

While they were talking, a sadhu was roaming in the compartment. The sadhu was wearing saffron robes. His hairs were appearing like the ropes of jute which were tied in huge bun on the top of his head. His long beards were almost covering his chest. His forehead was smeared with cream-colored marks of sandalwood paste. Those marks were in the shape of three horizontal and parallel lines. He was wearing a necklace of big beads of rudraksh. He was also carrying a kamandal which was made of dry shell of a medium-sized pumpkin. The sadhu was making a small stopover near each passenger and was asking for some alms. He was promising all sorts of boons from the almighty in lieu of the alms. Most of the people were not in a mood to listen to him. They did not even bother to look at him. Most of the people must have seen numerous begging sadhus in the train and at public places. Unperturbed by the indifferent attitude of people, he was going on in his task like any other person dedicated to his job. After some time, the sadhu was standing near that lady.

The sadhu turned towards that lady and said, "Gracious lady has been blessed with a male child. The god will always shower bounty on you. You will be endowed with many children and a happy and prosperous family. You should give some alms to this sadhu as a token of gratitude to the almighty."

The lady was trying to look down on the floor of the compartment as she was not confident of directly staring at the sadhu. With folded hands, she said, "I beg your pardon, baba. I am too poor to give any alms. Please forgive me for all my sins."

The sadhu thundered, "If you want your son to grow up to become a healthy youth, part with some money. Even a piece of jewelry would do. You are fortunate to come face to face with a great sadhu like me."

The lady did not say anything. She had just folded her hands and was staring at the floor. The sadhu waited for some moment. After that, the sadhu moved his hands like lightning. He snatched the fifty rupee note from the child's hand. Everybody was stunned at seeing that act of daylight robbery. It was like snatching a favorite toy from a child's hands. The child started crying. His mother started sobbing. Her sob soon turned into wailing. She said, "You are not a sage but a demon in the garb of a sage. The god must be looking at your act. You are sure to go to hell after your death. The note was gifted by his nana so that I could buy some jalebis for my child. You should be ashamed of depriving a child of the joy."

But the lady was unable to muster up courage to take her money back from the sadhu. Bujhaavan and his friends were also silent and were blankly staring at each other. The members of the family; in front of Bujhaavan; preferred to look the other way. The students showed as if they did not notice anything. Many of them were staring at the screens of their smartphones. But god was probably observing that dastardly act of the sadhu. He sent a savior in the form of the peanut seller; who was coming back after making rounds in other compartments. When the peanut seller understood what was going on, he began throwing some choicest swear words at the sadhu. After that, he snatched the note from the sadhu and gave it back in the hands of the child. Then he said to the sadhu, "Run for your life, otherwise I will throw you out of this train."

The sadhu swiftly left the compartment. People began to shout, "Bravo! You are really great. You have shown the courage which none of us could show. You deserve a round of applause."

Hearing a round of applause for him, the peanut seller shyly smiled and said, "It is nothing. I get to witness similar incidents almost on a daily basis.

Meanwhile, the train was approaching the city of Muzaffarpur. Looking outside the window, Bujhaavan said, "Hey Jitan, it looks like the road from Patna."

Jitan said, "Yeah, the flyover going above is the Assam road which goes via Samastipur. It means that we are about to reach Muzaffarpur. "

Bujhaavan said, "This also means that we will reach Darbhanga by tonight and there will be no need to spend another night in the train."

But the train stopped just after passing through under the flyover. It was a small railway station. Bujhaavan said, "It appears that someone has pulled the chain so that he can get down at his doorstep."

One of the students said, "They may have disconnected the hosepipe. A hosepipe connects the vacuum break system of two adjacent compartments. Brakes are automatically applied once you remove the hosepipe."

Bujhaavan said, "You appear to be an expert on a train's technology."

Another student said, "No, no, we are not experts on train's technology. We are experts at disconnecting the hosepipe. When we were studying in higher secondary school, we must have disconnected the hosepipes many times just for the kick of it. Sometimes, we also did it to stop the train near our school; in order to attend the classes on time."

The third student said, "When you will travel on the Mansi Saharsa section, many milk vendors disconnect hosepipes to stop the train. They don't allow the train to move until they are through with loading their milk containers."

Narayan was listening to their gibberish with rapt attention. He said with a certain degree of enthusiasm, "Bhaiya, can you train me in the skill of disconnecting the hosepipe? I will try it on the Delhi metro trains."

Hearing that, one of the students said, "I am not sure about the technology being used in Delhi metro but I am sure about one thing. The security staffs will immediately put you behind the bars. Don't even try it while you are in Delhi. But you can safely practice it in Bihar."

While they were discussing about the merits and demerits of chain pulling, the train began to move towards Muzaffarpur station. Bujhaavan said, "Hey Jitan, you can get fish fry at Muzaffarpur station. They make really tasty fish fry."

Jitan said, "Once we reach our village, I will catch many fishes from the river. I will give you a chance to feast on the fish for free. No need to waste our money here. You never know when a ticket checker or a policeman will come to ask for some pocket money in lieu of allowing your tricycle."

Hearing that, Bujhaavan lit a beeri and took a deep puff from it. Jitan, Ramchander and Narayan followed the suit by taking out their own beeris.

By the time they finished smoking, the train was leaving Muzaffarpur station. Once the train had crossed the eastern cabin and the subsequent crossings, the relative density of buildings was becoming low. The rows of houses were now interspersed with empty plots; indicating that it was a new development in the town. The city must be expanding in that direction as well. Most of the new houses were made in a way that their ground floors were at least ten feet high from the land. Some makeshift bridges; made of bamboo; were connecting the entrance of those houses with a pot-holed road passing through the area. After a while, the rows of sparse houses gave way to farmlands and orchards along the railway track. Most of the orchards were full of mango and litchi trees. Plenty of litchi trees can only be seen around Muzaffarpur as it is among the few places which are famous for litchis.

The train was running at good speed; as it passed through numerous smaller stations. After about an hour, the train came to a halt somewhere near Samastipur. The train must have stayed at that small station for about thirty minutes; indicating no vacancy at the platforms of Samastipur railway station.

Finally, the train resumed its journey and began moving towards Samastipur. Within five minutes, rows of pucca houses could be seen along the railway tracks; indicating that the train was entering an urban area. A cinema hall was visible on the left side of a railway crossing. Most of the bikes, auto-rickshaws and cars were jostling for space near the railway crossing. Bujhaavan said, "Jitan, the name of this cinema hall is Bhola talkies. Can you recall, we had come here to watch the hit movie Sholay?"

Jitan said, "Yeah, I think it was about five years ago. I still remember many dialogues from the movie."

The train was moving at a snail's pace; as it had to change many tracks while approaching the railway station. A motley crowd had gathered around a fish seller on the right side of the track. The stench of stale fish was coming inside the compartment. Many ladies in the compartment had covered their nose to avoid the stench. After that, the train crossed a small temple of Hanuman; followed by a tomb. The temple's walls were painted in orange, while the tomb was painted in green. Some devotional song could be heard from the loudspeaker atop the temple. Many people threw coins towards the temple and folded their hands in reverence to one of the popular Hindu gods. After that, the train was almost near the platform; which was indicated by the presence of numerous railway tracks spanning the width of about 500 meter. The train finally reached Samastipur at about half past four. The compartment had become almost vacant as many people got down from the train. Some men and women could be seen loading huge baskets and gunny sacks in the compartment. Those baskets and gunny sacks were full of vegetables. They were utilizing every empty space in the compartment to shove their stock of vegetables.

Bujhaavan said, "The train's stoppage is a little bit longer at this station. They will change the engine. The engine will be attached to another end of the train and our train will move in reverse direction from this station."

Narayan said, "Let us go to see how they connect the engine. I have never seen it."

Bujhaavan said, "Be careful and keep a watch on the time. You can take Ramchander along with you."

While Narayan and Ramchander had been to watch the engine, Bujhaavan and Jitan had nothing to do to kill their time. Bujhaavan said to Jitan, "Hey, can you make some tobacco for us?"

Jitan promptly took out the small plastic box of tobacco. He took out a few pinches of chopped leaves of tobacco and mixed a pinch of lime in it. Then he started mixing them with all the dedication befitting his favorite indulgence.

After finishing his task, Jitan offered half of the mixture to Bujhaavan and took the remaining portion in his mouth.

When Jitan was aiming to spit through the window, he saw a sort of commotion on the platform. People were running in all directions. He yelled at Bujhaavan, "Hey, look what is happening. It appears as if an earthquake or cyclone is going to hit us."

Bujhaavan tried to understand the situation. Within a few moments, the reason of the commotion could be clear. A bull was rampaging through the platform. People were running to save their life. While some people were gathered near the gates of the compartment, most of the people were clinging to the windows to see the horrible spectacle. The scared people were running ahead; followed by the bull. The bull was; in turn; being chased by a handful of policemen, some coolies and some vendors. After about ten minutes, the bull could be successfully chased away from the platform.

After that, Bujhaavan appeared to be worried. He said, "There is no sign of Ramchander and Narayan. I hope they are all right."

Jitan said, "Don't worry about them. They have long experience of herding the cows and buffaloes."

After about ten minutes of that incident, some policemen came with Ramchander and Narayan. Each guy was being carried by two policemen. Both Ramchander and Narayan were in bad shape; with bruises all over their body. Their clothes had been torn into tatters. Their wounds were oozing with blood. Anybody could easily understand that they had been gored by the bull. But they were conscious enough to tell about their coach number and fellow passengers.

Ramchander and Narayan were laid on their births. After that, the policemen were venting their anger on Bujhaavan and Jitan, "What was the need for taking a stroll on the platform? You should have prevented these guys from venturing out from the compartment."

Bujhaavan did not say anything, but Jitan said to the policemen, "Sir, it would have been better if they were given some medicine."

The policemen fumed, "Do you think you are in a hospital? You should thank us for bringing them to you. You can always take them to a doctor once you reach Darbhanga."

Hearing that, one of the students interrupted, "But I think the railway should provide some first-aid to these guys. Why does the railway have so many hospitals and doctors? Are they only meant for the staffs of the railway?"

One of the policemen replied, "Listen to them. They are talking like experts after reading a few books in their colleges. Just shut your mouth otherwise I will gore you the way that bull had gored them."

After that the policemen left the scene. Finally, the train left Samastipur at about half past five. It was now going in reverse direction. Bujhaavan shouted in joy, "Now, nobody can stop me from reaching Darbhanga tonight."

Hearing that, Jitan said, "But we have to go beyond Darbhanga and there is no bus for our village after six. We will have to spend the whole night at Darbhanga railway station. Taking care of two injured persons is an additional headache."

Ramchander was moaning in pain, "Can we go to some Dharmshala? We can get the much needed rest."

Narayan said, "Yeah, don't worry about the doctor or medicine. We will get medicine after reaching our village."

Bujhaavan said, "Staying at the station involves expenses. You need to eat something for dinner. You also need to pay some bribe to the policemen and ticket checker otherwise they don't allow you to enjoy a sound sleep."

Jitan said, "It is still cheaper than staying in a dharmshala (lodge)."

Bujhaavan said, "You are right, the dharmshala charges one hundred rupees per person per night, while you need to pay just a couple of hundreds to the railway staffs. You also get the facility of tea-sellers and beeri sellers throughout the night."

Jitan said, "We may get some painkillers for them. Some shops at the platform sell some general medicines."

Indicating towards his right, Jitan said, "Bujhaavan, I think it is the sugar mill. One of my relatives works at this sugar mill. He is the cousin of my nephew's brother-in-law. He gets all the comforts of a government job. He is lucky enough to be allotted a quarter in the sugar mill premises."

Hearing that, one of the students said, "But I have heard that the staffs of this sugar mill have not been paid salary since a long time."

Jitan said, "My relative makes his ends meet by siphoning off some sugar from the backdoor. Many staffs are involved in this affair. They are not earning too much but it is enough to live for another day."

By the time the train crossed the railway bridge over the Gandak, it was getting dark. The train stopped at Muktapur station. Bujhaavan said, "This must be Muktapur. I can recognize any station on this route even on a pitch dark night. This route had been my playground when I was a teenager. "

Jitan said, "You are probably talking of those days when you were working for some grocer at Darbhanga."

Bujhaavan said, "Yes, I had to make frequent rounds of the wholesale markets of Hayaghat and Samastipur to buy vegetables. It is not easy to transport vegetables through train but it is cheaper."

Narayan appeared to be curious to know the details. He asked, "Does the railway charge less for carrying vegetables?"

Bujhaavan said, "I am not aware about the charges. We used to load the vegetables in passenger trains. Then we had to deal with the ticket checkers and policemen throughout the way. But it was easier to finalize a deal with the guard."

Jitan asked, "How come?"

Bujhaavan said, "Once you get some space in the guard's compartment, you can easily load vegetables in that compartment. Then you get the luxury to deal with a single greedy person. It is always better than dealing with at least half a dozen greedy persons."

Meanwhile, one could hear constant sounds of clanging of metal against metal. Many people were suspending large metallic cans of milk to the grills of the windows. They were really swift and brutal while doing so. They did not even bother to look if someone was getting hit or injured from the metallic hooks dangling from the handle of the milk cans. Two cans of milk were suspended from the grill of each window of the compartment. It was duly followed by one bicycle being suspended from the grill of each window. None of the passengers raised an eyebrow; not to talk about protesting the sudden obstruction to their comfort zone.

After about five minutes, a train came from the opposite direction and crossed their train in a jiffy. The line between

Samastipur and Darbhanga is a single line which necessitates the stoppage of one train to allow a smooth passage to another train coming from the opposite direction.

One of the students said, "Let us see how many stoppages we will have to endure to allow the crossing of other trains."

Another student said, "In fact, this is the time of departure of many long distance trains from Darbhanga. Our train will get many opportunities to take the much needed breaks. It must be tired after covering a distance of more than a thousand kilometer."

After a couple of stopovers at smaller stations and many more crossings of trains, the train finally reached Laheriasarai at about seven. It is a small station and is at the doorstep of Darbhanga. Bujhaavan said, "Do you know that all big officials have their offices and residences at Laheriasarai? There is a straight road from this station which passes through the residences of SP (Superintendent of Police), Commissioner and DM (District Magistrate)."

Jitan said, "Yes I know. Once I got a chance to go to the residence of the DM. A person from my village is working as a peon at that place. The house is really big; looks like a palace. Ferocious looking security guards will welcome you at the gate. It is another story that they did not welcome me. There is a huge garden inside the boundary wall."

Narayan said, "Bhaiya, how can a person become a DM?"

One of the students said, "One needs to study a lot to become a DM. It is a tough examination. I am planning to prepare for that examination."

Meanwhile, the train was still at Laheriasarai station even after a long duration of more than half an hour. People were getting restless and were cursing the station master of Laheriasarai. It was the typical restlessness which anybody experiences because of the unnecessary delays at the eleventh hour.

Someone was telling, "I have to go near medical college. Had I been aware about this delay, I could have taken a rickshaw from Laheriasarai. I would have been at my home by now."

Another person told, "But I have heard that it is not safe to get down at this station once it becomes dark. This is a scary place. There is the risk of getting looted by hooligans."

Finally, the train left Laheriasarai station and reached Darbhanga in less than five minutes. Each passenger heaved a sigh of relief at the sight of glowing neon lights of the platform. Nobody was showing a hurry to get down from the train. They had all the time to quietly collect their luggage before saying a goodbye to the train which had been their home, their playground, their club, their restaurant; for the last thirty six hours.

Narayan and Ramchander were helped by Bujhaavan and Jitan to get down from the compartment. They found a suitable place at the platform and made comfortable bed for Ramchander and Narayan. Bujhaavan was able to find some painkillers from a shop at the platform.

While Narayan was taking the medicine, Bujhaavan said, "I am afraid the bull must have seen your red undergarment."

Jitan laughed and said, "The bull must have mistaken them for cows."

All of them laughed aloud.

As per the railway time table, the total journey time from New Delhi to Darbhanga is about twenty hours. Thus, the train was delayed by more than thirty hours. If the waiting time at New Delhi is included then the passengers from Delhi had to go through the ordeal for almost fifty hours. But the sense of reaching the destination was powerful enough for the passengers to look forward for numerous means and ways to reach their homes.

22142912R00193

Printed in Poland
by Amazon Fulfillment
Poland Sp. z o.o., Wrocław